I0649422

Alfred Cooper Fryer

Cuthberht of Lindisfarne

His Life and Times

Alfred Cooper Fryer

Cuthberht of Lindisfarne
His Life and Times

ISBN/EAN: 9783337053871

Printed in Europe, USA, Canada, Australia, Japan

Cover: Foto ©Raphael Reischuk / pixelio.de

More available books at **www.hansebooks.com**

Now Ready, Crown 8vo, Cloth, 3s. 6d.

CUTHBERHT OF LINDISFARNE:

His Life and Times.

By ALFRED C. FRYER, F.R.H.S., F.C.S.,

Associate of the British Archæological Association.

PRESS NOTICES.

" Written in a graphic, interesting, and varied style ; and thus an era in the ecclesiastical history of our empire, which is little known, is lucidly and eloquently portrayed."

Border Advertiser.

"This is a book Churchmen and antiquaries will delight to read."—*Derbyshire Courier.*

"Its perusal must arouse feelings of thankfulness in the mind of every intelligent reader, that the days of such gross darkness and superstition have for ever passed."—*Record.*

" Readers with a liking for antiquarian lore will be repaid by a perusal of " Cuthberht of Lindisfarne."—*Christian.*

"In many passages the language is very fine, such as the account of the death of the Venerable Bæda, his biographer."

Berwick Advertiser.

P. T. OVER.

PRESS NOTICES—continued.

"The author deserves our gratitude for the perseverance and care with which he has gathered together the particulars relating to the 'Patron Saint of Durham.' "—*The Friend.*

"We heartily commend the work, not only as providing an admirable account of the life of the saintly apostle, but also as throwing much light upon the religious events of the times in which he lived."—*Edinburgh Daily Review.*

"Whoever wishes for a lucid narrative of the events, and an adequate biographical sketch, of the eminent Northumbrian Abbot and Bishop will find it in this monograph."
Manchester City News.

"The author's style is sober and scholarly, and affords evidence of a great deal of painstaking investigation."
Cheshire County News and Chronicle.

"A vivid picture of the reign of the Columban Church on the shores of Northumberland."—*Manchester Examiner.*

"The work is not only acceptable as a record of St. Cuthberht's life; it also presents a careful study of the times and manners of his era."—*Scotsman.*

"Elegantly bound and cleverly written."—*Durham Chron.*

"We are much pleased with this book. In a quiet, pleasing way it word-paints the scenery of Cuthberht's and Bæda's Christian living."—*Churchman.*

This is an extremely well-meaning book, and obviously the writer has taken a good deal of trouble over it."—*Athenæum.*

"The author, by deep research, has caught the spirit of the age on which he writes, and gives us a series of graphic pictures of the religious progress of the seventh century."
Durham Chronicle.

LONDON: S. W. PARTRIDGE & Co., 9, PATERNOSTER ROW.

CUTHBERHT OF LINDISFARNE

CUTHBERHT OF LINDISFARNE

His Life and Times

BY

ALFRED C. FRYER, F.R.Hist.Soc.

LONDON

S. W. PARTRIDGE & CO., 9 PATERNOSTER ROW

1880

" How beautiful your presence, how benign,
  Servant of God ! who not a thought will share
  With the vain world ; who, outwardly as bare
  As winter trees, yield no fallacious sign
  That the firm soul is clothed with fruit divine !
  Such priest, when service worthy of his care
  Has called him forth to breathe the common air,
  Might seem a saintly image from the shrine
  Descended :—happy are the eyes that meet
  The apparition ; evil thoughts are stayed
  At his approach, and low-bowed necks entreat
  A benediction from his voice or hand ;
  Whence grace, through which the heart can understand
  And vows, that bind the will, in silence made."
                                    —WORDSWORTH.

PREFACE.

IN these pages is presented a concise account of Cuthberht, the saintly apostle of Northumbria, with some sketches of those associated in his mission. The times in which Cuthberht lived have been described somewhat fully. In obtaining some of his materials, the author has been indebted to Dr Greenwood and the other Trustees of Owen's College. From the Rev. Professor Bright, of Oxford, and the Rev. Dr Charles Rogers, of the Royal Historical Society, he has received help and encouragement. To the Rev. J. F.

Fowler he is indebted for permission to make free use of his work on St Cuthberht's Window in York Minster. Finally, he has to acknowledge his obligations to Mr J. D. Crichton, of London, for verifying references, and other useful assistance.

ELM HIRST, NEAR WILMSLOW,
CHESHIRE, *November* 1880.

CONTENTS.

CUTHBERHT OF LINDISFARNE.

CHAPTER I.

THE BIOGRAPHERS OF CUTHBERHT—BÆDA.

"O Venerable Bede!
The saint, the scholar, from a circle freed
Of toil stupendous, in a hallowed seat
Of learning, where thou heard'st the billows beat
On a wild coast—rough monitors to feed
Perpetual industry.   Sublime recluse !
The recreant soul, that dares to shun the debt
Imposed on human kind, must first forget
Thy diligence, thy unrelaxing use
Of a long life, and in the hour of death
The last dear service of thy passing breath."
—WORDSWORTH.

RESPECTING the two biographers of St Cuthberht, from whose works the materials presented in the following pages are chiefly derived, little is known. Of the earlier, a monk of Lindisfarne, not even the name has been preserved ; but by

Bæda, who wrote at a later date, his narrative was used. Both biographers had one qualification in common—they were contemporaries of the great bishop whom they celebrated, Bæda being, at the time of St Cuthberht's decease in 687, fourteen years old.

Monkton,[1] a hamlet in the parish of Jarrow-on-Tyne, claims honour as the birthplace of Bæda. There in 673[2] was born this venerable father of the Anglo-Saxon Church. His parents' names are unknown, but he describes himself as "born of a noble stock of the Angles." Bæda was early devoted to a religious life, for at the tender age of seven he entered the monastery of St Peter at Wearmouth, under care of the abbot. Respecting his instructor, Benedict Biscop, Bæda, with a touch of that drollery which characterised the monastic writers of his

---

[1] A well at Monkton is still known by Bæda's name (History of Durham, by Robert Surtees, Lond., 1816).

[2] For the controversy respecting the precise date of Bæda's birth, see Giles' Life of Bæda, p. 6.

period, writes thus : "He was a man of venerable life, blessed (*benedictus*) both in grace and in name, . . . surpassing his age by his manners, and addicted to no false pleasures. He was descended of a noble lineage of the Angles, and, by a corresponding dignity of mind, worthy to be exalted into the company of the angels."[1] Benedict Biscop was brought up at the court of King Oswin. Unwearied in the pursuit of learning and zealous for the welfare of his country, on five occasions he visited Rome, each time bringing with him some valuable collections. In his train came masons and glaziers, who instructed his countrymen in the art of church building. By Benedict the monastery of Wearmouth was founded, and within its walls Bæda grew up. There Trumhere, disciple of Chad,[2] and Sigfrid, a pupil of St Cuth-

---

[1] Bæda, Hist. Eccles., Ann. Abbat.

[2] Bæda, Hist. Eccles., iv. 3. Chad or Ceadda was a missionary bishop among the Mercians. The see of Lichfield was dedicated to his memory. In 669 he was succeeded in the archbishopric of York by Wilfrith.

berht, were his teachers in theology. By
John the arch-chanter, who had accompanied Benedict from Rome, he was instructed in music. And, though it has not
been recorded, it is probable that the knowledge of Greek and Latin, for which he was
renowned, may have been acquired under
the tuition of a pupil of Archbishop Theodore[1] and his friend Adrian. A cultivator
of classical learning, Bæda manifested genius
in other fields. He acquired a knowledge
of geography, history, and medicine, also of
the exact sciences. In his native tongue
he composed extensively, but of these com-
positions none remain.

When Ceolfrid was appointed to the
charge of Jarrow—an offshoot from the
monastery of Wearmouth—Bæda, yet a
boy, accompanied the new abbot. The
old church of St Paul at Jarrow, erected

---

[1] Theodore of Tarsus, a Greek monk, sent to Britain
from Rome in 668, became Archbishop of Canterbury.
From him the Church of England took life and form.
He died in 690.

about 685,[1] stood on the right bank of the
Tyne, three miles to the south-west of South
Shields. By Grose the antiquary its situa-
tion has been described thus :

> " . . . Salt weed and stinking ooze,
> Most like the drowsy flood which poets feign
> Dark Styx, with wreaths of moistful osier hung."

But other writers have dwelt on the quiet
beauty of the scene. On the side of a
grassy knoll which rises above the river's
bank stands the venerable ruin. In the
foreground a disused haven, known as the
" slake," is said to have floated the fleet of
King Ecgfrith. Round the base of the hill
cluster pit-men's cottages, and in the distance the chimneys and shipping of South
Shields break the line of the horizon.

Bæda began at Jarrow a course of study
which he continued upwards of fifty years.
In the quiet of its monastic cell he qualified

---

[1] The inscription on the dedication stone bears that
the edifice was erected in the fifteenth year of King
Ecgfrith, *i.e.*, 685. The name of Ceolfrid is mentioned
as abbot and founder.

himself as a religious teacher. It was his life-work to labour for the glory of God and the good of his fellow-men; and from first to last he walked consistently. His was a quiet, uneventful career, yet underneath its calm exterior were hidden strong forces, and his influence was destined to be felt, not only in the narrow circle of his associates, but by his age and country.

Roused at dawn by the convent bell, young Bæda would repair to the little church and chant the matin hymn. We can almost hear the fresh young voice repeat the words of David: "Teach me, O Lord, the way of Thy statutes, and I shall keep it unto the end. Give me understanding, and I shall keep Thy law." The day begun with praise was passed in study, and the evensong went up from a thankful heart.

The quiet routine of his "cniht-hood,"[1] the term by which was expressed the period between infancy and adolescence, was broken by a sad event. A fatal pestilence had swept

[1] Turner's History of the Anglo-Saxons, iii. 18.

away all in the little community who could read, preach, or chant, except the Abbot Ceolfrid and a small boy who had been trained by him.[1] Discontinued at first save at matins and vespers, the services were afterwards chanted in full by Ceolfrid and the young neophyte until they were joined by competent assistants.

Bæda was ordained a deacon at an early age. He writes thus: "In the nineteenth year of my age I received deacon's orders, in the thirtieth those of the priesthood, both of them under the ministry of the most reverend Bishop John, and by order of the Abbot Ceolfrid."[2]

It seems nearly certain that Bæda never wandered far from the congenial quiet of his Northumbrian home.[3] Of kindness received from Wictred, King of Kent, he makes record; he also refers to a visit

[1] Hist. Ann. Abbat., Bædæ Opera, vi. 421.

[2] Bæda, Hist. Eccles., v. 24. The ecclesiastic referred to was John of Beverley, Bishop of Hexham.

[3] For an account of Bæda's supposed journey to Rome, see Lives of Eminent Anglo-Saxons, p. 165.

which he paid to Ecgberht, Archbishop of York.[1] Of Ceolwulf of Northumbria, a prince of considerable learning, he was a favoured guest; his " Ecclesiastical History" was composed at the request of that potentate, and the manuscript was submitted to his review. Subsequent to Bæda's death, Ceolwulf abandoned the regal dignity, and sought retirement in the monastery of Lindisfarne.

Like missionaries of later times, Bæda took part in outdoor labour. Of this side of conventual life he has left us a picture in describing the pious abbot who assisted Benedict at Wearmouth. " Frequently as he went forth," writes Bæda, " on the business of the monastery, if he found the brethren working, he would join them and work with them, taking the plough-handle or wielding the fore-hammer, or winnowing the grain." [2]

---

[1] Bæda's Letters to Wictred and Ecgberht.

[2] Bæda, Hist. Eccles., Ann. Abbat., v. ; see also his account of Abbot Easterwine, who exchanged the court of King Ecgfrith for a monastic cell.

Outside the walls of Jarrow stirring events were taking place. War ravaged the land, and the Northumbrian dynasty tottered to its fall. Bæda's cell was undisturbed by the storm that raged without.[1] Hymns, homilies, Scriptural commentaries, lives of the saints, and disquisitions on grammar and chronology flowed from his busy pen. "My own secretary," he records, "I make my own notes, and am my own librarian." Not confined to the duties of the desk, he was a diligent teacher. Attracted by his learning, a school of monks was established at Jarrow. Having composed his "Life of St Cuthberht,"[2] he dedicated the

---

[1] About a year before his death, Bæda, in a letter to Archbishop Ecgberht of York, proposed a vigorous and statesmanlike plan of reform; but it came too late.

[2] An excellent translation of Bæda's Life of St Cuthberht will be found in the Historical Tracts of Venerable Bæda, edited by the Rev. A. Giles, D.C.L. Bæda wrote two biographies of St Cuthberht, one in prose, the other in verse. Of his metrical narrative, which is composed in vigorous hexameters, the following is a specimen:

" Multa suis Dominus fulgescere lumina seclis
Donavit, tetricas humanæ noctis ut umbras

B

work to Bishop Eadfrid.   He was careful
about his authorities.   In his preface he men-
tions how he had frequently submitted the
manuscript to Herefrid the Priest, and to
others who were personally familiar with
the subject of it.

Bæda's " Ecclesiastical   History,"   the
greatest monument of his genius, was composed in the true spirit of historical inquiry.
Drawn from various sources, not the least
interesting portion is that bearing on con-
temporaneous events.   It was completed
just three years before the author's decease.

Bæda's end was near ;[1] incessant toil had
begun to affect his strength.   About Easter
735, a severe attack of asthma, attended
with great debility, interrupted his course of

Lustraret divina poli de culmine flamma ;
Et licet ipse deo natus de lumine Christus
Lux sit summa, Deus sanctos quoque jure lucernæ
Ecclesiæ rutilare dedit, quibus igne magistro
Sensibus instet amor, sermonibus æstuat ardor
Multifidos varium lychnos qui sparsit in orbem ;
Ut cunctum nova lux fidei face fusa sub axem
Omnia sidereis virtutibus arva repleret."

[1] For an account of Bæda's last days, see Cuthberht's
letter to Cuthwine.

study. Nevertheless he laboured on, evincing the same cheerful humour which distinguished him alike in sickness and in health. His infirmities increased. Night brought no refreshing slumber ; and·in the weariness of prostration he was heard to repeat the great apostle's words, " It is a fearful thing to fall into the hands of the living God." More frequently were on his lips the verses of an English song.

> " Before the journey that we all must go
> There is no man, though thoughtful ever so,
> That can discover, ere he pass the gates,
> What doom, or good or evil him awaits." [1]

To the reading and singing of his pupils he listened eagerly. "By turns," writes his biographer, " we read, and by turns we wept ; nay, we wept always whilst we read. In such joy we passed the days of Lent, and he rejoiced much, and gave God thanks, because he had been thought worthy to be so weakened." Among the antiphones

[1] Professor W. J. Hale's translation—Conversion of the West—The English, by the Rev. Dr Maclear, p. 150.

chanted for his comfort was the one for Ascension Day.[1] At the touching words, "Leave us not orphans," the pupils and their master wept together. The torch of life still flickered feebly, and the dying man lingered wishful only to finish his translation of St John's Gospel. On the Tuesday before Ascension Day an increased difficulty in breathing showed that the end was near. Dictating to his amanuensis, he referred to his waning energy. Another morning found him still alive, with only a single chapter wanting to complete his task. "Dearest master," said the scribe, "there lacks but one chapter; yet it will but trouble thee to put more questions." "It is easily done," was the reply; "take thy pen, make ready,

---

[1] In the Sarum Breviary this antiphon was used at the vesper service for Ascension Day. With a slight alteration it is still retained in the liturgy of the Church of England, and forms a portion of the service for the Sunday after Ascension. The word "orphans" of the original, which had such a touching significance to the pupils of the dying Bæda, is in the modern version rendered "comfortless."

and write fast." At noon his fellow-priests of the monastery were summoned, and on each he bestowed some small gift as a memorial. The shadows were deepening, and the hour of even-song was drawing nigh, when the last sentence was penned. " The verse is now finished, master," said the scribe. " Truly hast thou said, it is finished," responded the master. " Take now my head between thy hands, and place me opposite the spot where I was wont to pray, that I may call upon the Father." Stretched on the pavement of his cell, he chanted the doxology, "Glory to the Father," and as the last note ceased, his spirit passed away.

" The lamp of learning," writes Surtees, " trimmed by the hand of a simple monastic who never passed the limits of his Northumbrian province, irradiated from the cell of Jarrow the Saxon realm of England with a clear and steady light; and, when Bæda died, History reversed her torch, and quenched it in deep night."

CHAPTER II.

" Servants of God! or sons
Shall I not call you? because
Not as servants ye knew
Your Father's innermost mind,
His, who unwillingly sees
One of His little ones lost—
Yours is the praise, if mankind
Hath not as yet in its march
Fainted, and fallen, and died! "
—M. ARNOLD.

ABOUT a mile and a half distant from the Northumbrian coast, but connected with the mainland by a narrow isthmus, is the island of Lindisfarne, interesting to the student of history from its association with the names of Aidan and Cuthberht.

The date of Aidan's birth has not been recorded; a noble and even royal lineage has been claimed for him. A native of

Ireland, he sprung from the regal stock of Eochaidh Finn, of which St Brigid was a collateral descendant.[1] His name was borne by several Irish and Dalriadic kings.[2] He appears first as a monk of Iona.

In the year 634, the inmates of Hii, as this Columban settlement was designated, were assembled in solemn chapter to receive a delegate from Oswald, King of Northumbria. They were called on to make an important decision. Desirous of fostering religion and the arts of peace, Oswald, who had lately recovered his sceptre, had invited missionaries from Iona to settle in his dominions, assuring them of his protection. For his request there was a special cause. At Iona the young prince, after the death of his father Ethelfrith, had, with other

[1] Dr Forbes' Kalendar of Scottish Saints, Edin., 1872, 4to, p. 269.

[2] Forbes' Lives of St Ninian and St Kentigern, Edin., 1874, 8vo, p. lxxv.; Reeves' Life of St Columba, Edin., 1874, 8vo, pp. 254, 264, 287; Laing's Cronykel of Wyntown, Edin., 1879, 8vo, p. 324; Burton's Hist. Scot., i. 279.

members of the family, sought refuge from
the usurper Eadwin, receiving in the monastery shelter and hospitality.   During
his residence he became a convert to the
Christian faith.[1]

These events happened in the year 617,
during the incumbency of Fergna, the fourth
abbot ;[2] but in the lapse of seventeen years
important changes had occurred.   Eadwin
had extended his sway northwards to the
Forth, while all the Saxon states south of
Northumbria, Kent excepted, had submitted
to his authority.   In the train of his second
wife, Ethelburga, daughter of Ethelberht,
the Christian monarch of Kent, came Paulinus, a zealous partisan of the church at
Canterbury.   Converted by the preaching
of this disciple of St Augustine, King Eadwin and his subjects publicly professed
the new faith; and the bishopric of York,
in 627, was founded for Paulinus.   Then
followed a golden age, when the land re-

[1] Bæda, Hist. Eccles., iii. 1.
[2] Skene's Celtic Scotland, ii. 153.

joiced under the rule of a law-abiding, truth-loving prince. But the happy period did not endure long. In 633 Eadwin fell in battle, defending his kingdom from the inroads of Penda, the pagan King of Mercia.[1] A period of anarchy followed. Abandoning his see, Paulinus fled to the Kentish court along with the widowed queen and her daughter; while James, "the deacon," was alone left to conduct religious service.[2]

Uniting his forces with the wild hordes of the Welsh king, Cadwallon, who, nominally a Christian, exceeded in barbarity his pagan ally, Penda ravaged the land with fire and sword.[3] In the words of Bæda, "no longer might the cups of brass hang safely by the roadside wells; or a woman with her babe traverse the kingdom of Eadwin from sea to sea, without dread of insult."[4]

[1] The locality of this conflict has been disputed; opinion being divided as to whether Heathfield, in Derbyshire, or Hatfield-Chase, in Yorkshire, was the scene of Eadwin's defeat.

[2] Bæda, Hist. Eccles., ii. 20.

[3] *Ibid.*, iii. 1.   [4] *Ibid.*, ii. 16.

To the terrors of invasion were added the horrors of civil war. Northumbria was split into the two provinces of Deira and Bernicia; of which the former fell to Osric, Eadwin's cousin; the latter to Eanfrith, one of the exiled sons of Ethelfrith. Both monarchs abandoned the Christian faith. Shortly afterwards they were slain by Cadwallon; and the path of succession to Oswald was thus opened up.

Mustering his forces, Oswald marched to attack the Welsh prince, who was encamped near Hexham. According to Camden, the two armies encountered at Dilston on an affluent of the Tyne; but later authors have identified the scene of conflict with St Oswald's, a village near the Roman Wall. The name of the engagement—Catscaul or Cad-ys-gual—the battle at the wall—as given by the old Cymric chroniclers, seems to favour the latter view.[1] Adamnan relates that during the night before the battle St Columba appeared in a vision to Oswald, and

[1] Skene's Celt. Scot., i. 245.

assured him of victory; and that the king told this story to Abbot Seghine.[1] A rudely-shaped wooden cross was planted in front of Oswald's position at Hefenfield; and, as the morning mist rolled up the vale of the Deniseburn, the king, with his host, knelt in prayer round the symbol of their faith.[2] The result of the conflict was decisive. Cadwallon perished with the flower of his army; and the power of Oswald was established in Northumbria on a firm basis.[3]

Oswald now directed his thoughts to the religious instruction of his people, and his former relations with Iona led him to solicit from that community competent teachers. Applying to Seghine, Abbot of Hii, he received from him a bishop named Corman.[4] But Corman was not destined to be the apostle of Northumbria. Of an austere

[1] Skene's Celt. Scot., i. 245; iii. 157.
[2] Bæda, Hist. Eccles., iii. 2.
[3] Turner's Hist. of the Anglo-Saxons, i. 359; Llywarch Hen's Elegy on Cadwallon, i. 121; Owen's Llywarch, pp. 111-117.
[4] Bæda, Hist. Eccles., iii. 5.

disposition, his preaching was ineffectual, and he quitted his post, disgusted with a failure which he attributed to his flock. As he denounced to the brethren the stubborn character of Oswald's subjects,[1] Aidan, a brother of the order, said, " Hast thou not dealt too severely with thine unlearned hearers, neglecting the apostle's advice to feed first with the milk of the Word, and afterwards with meat ? " Appointed by the brethren to renew the mission, and invested with the episcopal office, Aidan sailed from Iona in the summer of 635.[2]

Oswald greeted the new bishop warmly, and, at his request, transferred the seat of his episcopate from York to Lindisfarne. The island derived its name from a stream, the Lindis, which entered the sea at a point on the Northumbrian coast directly opposite, and from the Celtic word *fahren*—a recess,

---

[1] Bæda, Hist. Eccles., iii. 5.

[2] Lismore in Ireland, and Kingarth in Bute, two offshoots from the parent establishment at Iona, were ruled by bishops, and from one of these probably Aidan received consecration (Skene's Celt. Scot., ii. 157).

sufficiently indicative of its wild and se-
cluded character. The natural strength of
the position probably guided Aidan in
choosing the Holy Isle as his residence.
Connected with the mainland by a strip of
dry sand, the peninsula was, twice a day,
by the flow of the tide, converted into an
island;[1] thus defying attack by an enemy
unprovided with boats. Moreover, the royal
fortress of Bamborough[2] was distant only
an hour's sail.

In the south-western angle of the island
Aidan built his church, a simple structure
of oaken beams thatched with a species of
long coarse grass, which there grows plenti-
fully. Several brethren from Iona came as

[1] " For, with the flow and ebb, its style
  Varies from continent to isle ;
  Dry-shod, o'er sands, twice every day,
  The pilgrim to his shrine finds way ;
  Twice every day the waves efface,
  Of staves and sandalled feet, the trace."
                  —Scott, *Marmion*, c. ii. 9.

[2] Bamborough was originally called Bebbanburgh,
after Bebba, the wife of its founder, Ida.

his companions ;[1] these gave instruction in a school founded for twelve boys. Of Aidan's pupils three, Eata, Wilfrith, and Ceadda, became subsequently famous.[2]

In conducting the duties of his episcopate Aidan was independent both of Canterbury and of Rome. With doctrinal controversies he had no concern. To him it was nothing, that the Pope claimed the right of appointing an English archbishop to exercise supreme authority over other bishops.[3] Yet Rome, in recognising him as a missionary bishop, rendered justice to his self-sacrificing and zealous labours.

To those who courted retirement and loved contemplation, Lindisfarne, like the sea-girt Iona, offered an inviting retreat. But the lives of Aidan and his colleagues were not passed in seclusion. It was only by unremitting toil they could hope to sow the good seed ; and to their self-imposed task they applied themselves with unwearied dili-

---

[1] Bæda, Hist. Eccles., iii. 3.
[2] *Ibid.*, iii. 26.   [3] *Ibid.*, i. 27.

gence. Hunger, cold, poverty, vicissitudes
of every sort were familiar to them. Their
journeys were performed on foot; their fare
was meagre; their garb humble. Though
often the honoured guests of kings they remained men of lowly hearts and simple habits.
In the pages of Bæda and other contemporary
chroniclers, the "golden deeds" of Aidan
and his successors are lovingly recorded.

Aidan laboured for sixteen-years (from
634 to 651) among the sturdy race of dales-
men, fishermen, and miners, who formed the
population of Northumbria. From the
Humber to the Forth he traversed the land
on foot, teaching from house to house. On
these journeys he was frequently accompanied by King Oswald, who, from Aidan's
ignorance of the northern dialect, acted
as interpreter.[1] Favoured with the royal
countenance, his preaching was successful.
Christian doctrines were everywhere ac-
cepted; churches were built, monasteries

[1] Bæda, Hist. Eccles., iii. 3; Laing's Wyntoun, 1879,
iii. 325.

endowed. In his "Ecclesiastical History" Bæda has eloquently delineated the character of this missionary bishop. Peace-loving and charitable, he despised pomp, and was superior to avarice. Rebuking the proud with priestly authority he comforted the afflicted with Christian tenderness. In him the poor found a protector, one ready to plead their cause and relieve their wants. On the vexed question of Easter observance Bæda notes as a fault, that the practice of Aidan, as of all Scotic ecclesiastics, was at variance with that of Rome. Controversy on this subject raged keenly. The disciples of Columba were charged with error in celebrating the Christian festival on the full-moon of the Jewish passover. Respecting Aidan, however, Bæda explains that he held his Easter celebration on the first Sunday after the full moon: he further exonerates him on the ground of his remoteness from civilisation and consequent ignorance of canonical law.[1]

[1] Burton, Hist. Scot., i. 267, *et seq.*

"Yet," adds the candid historian, "this I approve in him that in the celebration of Easter the object which he had in view in all he said, did, or preached, was the same as ours, that is, the redemption of mankind through the passion, resurrection, and ascension into heaven of the man Jesus Christ."[1] A cultured scholar, reared in the school of Augustine, Bæda might differ polemically from the Celtic bishop; nevertheless, in the latter he recognised a kindred spirit, which rejoiced to promote the spread of the Gospel and the welfare of humanity.

A diligent student of Holy Scripture, Aidan encouraged others to search the Divine word. On his missionary journeys he prescribed to his attendants certain portions of the Psalter to be committed to memory. When invited to the royal table he brought with him as guests one or two of his clergy. Illustrative of his relations with King Oswald there are many legends. One Easter Sunday Oswald was feasting

[1] Bæda, Hist. Eccles., iii. 17.

with his nobles, and Aidan sat at his right
hand.   A silver dish heaped with choice
food had been placed before the king, when
the royal almoner approaching reported that
a number of poor people were sitting outside the palace gates begging. Oswald at
once handed the costly dish, its contents
untasted, to the thegn bidding him distribute
the viands among the poor, and then break
the vessel in pieces for their behoof. Aidan,
approving the act, blessed the king's " white
hand," exclaiming, " May it never grow
old." [1]

Temperate at table, Aidan was in all his
habits simple and unaffected. The gifts of
wealthy admirers he bestowed in alms, and
for the manumission of slaves he laboured
earnestly.   Of those who were rescued from
serfdom some were trained in his school,
and ordained as priests.[2] The conversion of
Northumbria made slow progress, though
fresh relays of Celtic missionaries were
despatched from Iona.   But ere the final

---

[1] Bæda, Hist. Eccles., iii. 6.   [2] *Ibid.*, iii. 5.

victory over heathendom was won the land had to pass through a fiery baptism.

Wessex had early succumbed to Oswald; and its ruler, having embraced the Christian faith, was in 635 baptized by Birinus, a Benedictine monk, who established a see at Dorchester, in Oxfordshire. In East Anglia about the same period Felix was preaching. The success of these missionaries awakened the apprehensions of Penda, King of Mercia, who probably dreaded a coalition, and in 642 his cruel hordes were again let loose upon the land. Convening his people, Oswald marched to the relief of his allies. On this occasion victory did not rest on the side of the cross. The autumn of 642 beheld the disaster of Hatfield-Chase repeated at Maserfield, and Penda again triumphed.[1] The precise locality of the battlefield is unknown. Makerfield, near Warrington, and Mirfield, in Yorkshire, have been suggested; but it is now generally agreed that it was in the neighbourhood of

[1] Bæda, Hist. Eccles., iii. 9.

Oswestry (Oswald's tree), in Shropshire, that the pagan and Christian hosts met on the fatal 5th of August. Oswald fell, uttering with his last breath a prayer for his faithful subjects. By order of his brutal victor, his body was dismembered, and his head, arms, and hands exposed on stakes. In the following year, when the wave of conquest had ebbed, the sad relics were piously collected and conveyed to Northumbria. The head, delivered to Aidan, was by him interred at Lindisfarne, while the feet and hands were deposited in St Peter's Church at Bamborough.[1]

Thus, in the flower of his age, perished King Oswald. His fervent piety and generous temper endeared him to his people. By the Church he was canonised. Tradition affirms that when the other portions of his body had decayed, the generous hand of the Northumbrian hero remained uncorrupted.[2]

With the death of Oswald the kingdom

[1] Bæda, Hist. Eccles., iii. 9.　　[2] *Ibid.*, pp. 9-13.

of Northumbria fell to pieces. His brother
Oswin succeeded to the sovereignty of
Bernicia, and married Eanfleda, a daughter
of King Edwin. Over Deira ruled Oswine,
son of Osric and cousin of Eadwin, whose
courtesy and affable disposition soon won
the hearts of his subjects, and attracted
strangers to his service.[1]

Northumbria continued to offer desperate
resistance to the inroads of Penda. Year
by year the Mercian king pushed his con-
quests further north. Once he encamped
before the citadel of Bamborough. But
the impregnable rock defied his efforts, and
as a last resource he sought to destroy the
stronghold by fire. By his directions a quan-
tity of combustibles — beams and rafters,
wattle and thatch, the spoil of the ruined
hamlets in the vicinity—was piled in a huge
semicircle round the walls, and fire applied.
Thick clouds of smoke and flame rolled
upwards, obscuring the sky. In his island
home at Lindisfarne Aidan beheld the con-

[1] Bæda, Hist. Eccles., iii. 14.

flagration, which, fanned by a seaward
breeze, threatened to envelop the fortress
and the wooden buildings of the city in a
common doom. Raising his clasped hands
in an agony of supplication, he ejaculated,
"See, Lord, what great harm Penda is
doing." Suddenly the wind veered, and,
blowing from the opposite quarter, beat
back the flames on those who were feeding
them. Bamborough was saved! and the
heathen host withdrew from assailing a
stronghold which seemed to be divinely
protected.[1]

To Oswine Bishop Aidan proved a true
friend and judicious counsellor; and the
young king bestowed on him many tokens
of regard. A story is related, which would
seem to show that the king's good-nature
was occasionally severely tried. A beggar
having asked alms of Aidan, the bishop with
impulsive generosity gave him a horse which
he had recently received as a gift from the
king. Vexed with the slight put upon his

[1] Bæda, Hist. Eccles., iii. 16.

favour, Oswine remonstrated. With Celtic quickness Aidan rejoined, "Is the horse more to thee, O Oswine, than a .son of God ?" The implied reproof sank into the king's sensitive heart, and he entreated forgiveness. "Never again," he exclaimed, "shall I judge how much or how little thou should'st bestow on the poor !" Touched by this proof of Oswine's humility, Aidan turned to a Celtic priest who accompanied him, and prophesied that so good and meek a king would not long survive.[1]

The sequel proved the truth of the bishop's utterance. The latent jealousy which had always existed between the kings of Bernicia and Deira revived, and at last they came to an open rupture. But Oswine, discovering that the forces of his rival were numerically superior, relinquished the intended contest ; and disbanding. his army at Wilfaresdun, near Catterick, sought refuge with Earl Hunwald. Proving faithless, the earl betrayed the fugitive king, with the thegn

. Bæda, Hist. Eccles., iii. 14.

Tondhere, his sole attendant, into the enemy's hands. By his rival's command the royal fugitive and his servant were put to death; but the deed left on Oswine's name a stain which his subsequent victories could not efface. Bæda has recorded his repentance, and at the request of his gentle consort, Oswine subsequently granted to Trumhere, a Northumbrian priest, and relative of the murdered king, a portion of land near the scene of the crime, on which a monastery was built.[1]

For Oswin Aidan obtained in marriage the daughter of Eadwin;[2] and he induced the famous Hild to settle in his dominions, within the diocese of Lindisfarne.[3] The convent over which she ruled as abbess was established at Heruten,[4] near the

---

[1] Oswine was succeeded by his son Adelwald, on whose death, in 655, were united under one sceptre the twin-kingdoms of Bernicia and Deira.

[2] Bæda, Hist. Eccles., iii. 15, 21.

[3] *Ibid.*, iii. 24; iv. 23.

[4] Hart Island. The convent cemetery was discovered in 1833, its site having been covered by a field.

mouth of the Tees, on the site of the modern town of Hartlepool. But the assassination of his royal friend and patron was Aidan's death-blow; he did not long survive the tragedy. Twelve days he lingered, mourning for the murdered prince, whom he had loved as a son; and then death released him. He expired at Bamborough on the last day of August 651.[1] His last illness attacked him with such a sudden severity that it was found impossible to remove him to his chamber; a tent was thereupon erected over him as he lay upon the ground. A post at the western end of Bamborough Church, on which the dying bishop leaned his head, was preserved as a sacred relic; it twice escaped destruction when the remainder of the edifice was burned.

In Scotland the memory of St Aidan was revered, and churches were dedicated to him at Cambusnethan and Menmuir; several wells, also supposed to exercise

---

[1] Bæda, Hist. Eccles., iii. 17.

healing virtues, bore his name.[1]   By his successor Finian, a chapel was erected at Lindisfarne, which was afterwards substantially repaired by Archbishop Theodore.[2]

Bishop Aidan's life was one of unceasing toil, for it was by sheer personal labour that he promoted Christianity in Northumbria. The root planted by him sprung up and flourished till it overshadowed the whole land. Bæda has dwelt on his unselfish spirit and missionary zeal, yet he was not singular in possessing these virtues, for they were common to all missionaries of the Columban Church. "I see them coming!" says an eloquent writer, "not counting their lives dear unto themselves, clad in the armour of purity and innocence, to contend with strong seas and barren shores. . . . I see them coming! the leader and his twelve undaunted associates and disciples! Happy number! like those of old who, by the power of the weakness of

[1] Forbes' Kalendar of Scottish Saints, p. 269.
[2] Bæda, Hist. Eccles., iii. 25.

God, trampled upon strength, and under the ignominious sign of the cross conquered the honourable world. They approach the shore; they land; the meek have taken possession of the unknown rock upon which their sandals tread. The cross, emblem of self-denial, agony, and shame, carries the armour of an invisible panoply. Onward advances the sacerdotal host. The isles obey; kingdoms are conquered; their word has gone out into all lands."[1] In this spirit Aidan and his successors went forth to preach; in this spirit they toiled; in this spirit they triumphed!

[1] Dr Gordon's Monasticon, i. 575.

CHAPTER III.

" And as the moon from some dark gate of cloud
Throws o'er the sea a floating bridge of light,
Across whose trembling planks our fancies crowd
Into the realm of mystery and night—
So from the world of spirits there descends
A bridge of light, connecting it with this ;
O'er whose unsteady floor, that sways and bends,
Wander our thoughts above the dark abyss."
—LONGFELLOW.

THE lamp of Christianity kindled in Aidan's rude cell was not extinguished when he ceased to live. His successors in Lindisfarne, Finian and Colman, maintained the struggle against paganism ; and the churches raised by his disciples continued to flourish. Somewhere between the years 634 and 651, the monasteries of Melrose and Coldingham, offshoots of the parent church at Lindisfarne, sprang into existence. The latter, situated on the coast of Berwick, was, like Heruten, an establishment both for monks and nuns ; it was ruled by its foundress Ebba, a sister of King Oswald. Over Melrose in 651, the year of Aidan's death, presided Eata, one of his twelve disciples.

But far away in Scotland a greater than Wilfrith or Eata was even then standing on the threshold of a glorious career, and preparing, though unconsciously to himself, to take up the great work of evangelisation where Aidan had laid it down. As the pious bishop passed from earth, his mantle descended, not on abbot or neophyte trained in the school of Lindisfarne, but on a humble shepherd, tending his flocks among the wild recesses of Lammermoor.

Legend and romance have so beclouded the early history of the British Church, that it is most difficult to distinguish between fact and fiction in the lives of ancient missionaries. To this remark the biography of the patron saint of Durham proves an exception. Bæda and the anonymous monk

of Holy Isle have preserved the actual
details of his career. But these details,
valuable as they are, do not furnish complete information. On the subject of Cuthberht's parentage Bæda is silent, commencing his prose memoir of the saint with an
anecdote relating to an occurrence which
took place when Cuthberht was about
eight years old. To supply the omission, a
mass of legends,[1] more or less fabulous,
were latterly interwoven with the saint's [2]
history.

[1] Libellus de ortu S. Cuthberti de historiis Hybernen-
sium. exceptus et translatus (Surtees, Soc. Publ., viii.
61-87).

[2] In York Minster an ancient window is still shown,
emblazoned with paintings illustrative of the legends connected with St Cuthberht ; and the events and miracles
of his life were depicted in chronological order on the
windows of Durham Abbey, between the church door
and the cloisters. In the cathedral of Durham, formerly,
among other inscriptions beneath the figures of Benedictine monks, delineated on the screen of the altar of St
Jerome and St Benedict, was the following : "Sanctus
Cuthbertus, patronus ecclesiæ, civitatis et libertatis Dunel-
mensis, natione Hibernicus, regiis parentibus ortus, nutu
Dei Angliam perductus, et apud Mailros monachus est

According to these romances of the twelfth century, Cuthberht was a native, not of England or Scotland, but of Ireland; and the place of his nativity is fixed at Kells, in county Meath. Respecting the Irish stories, Monsignor Eyre writes thus: "The origin and value of the evidence furnished in the Irish Life of St Cuthberht, and quoted from it by other writers, is discussed by the Bollandists, who have shown it to be full of anachronisms. Without rejecting it as fabulous, the author would suggest that the mistake has arisen from confounding the name of St Cuthberht with that of St Columba. St Columba was born of noble descent at Kells, in Meath, where his house is still shown, and where no tradition of any kind connected with St Cuthberht is known to exist."[1]

According to the "Book of Nativity,"

effectus, deinde in ecclesiam Lindisfarnensem per abbatem suum Eatam translatus," etc. (see Rites of Durham, pp. 65, 112).

[1] Eyre's History of St Cuthberht, p. 4.

Cuthberht was the son of Sabina, an Irish princess, who, after the slaughter of her relations, had fallen, as captive, to the share of the King of Connatha.[1] At the moment of his birth a wonderful light filled the house, which appeared to be wrapped in flames, yet unconsumed.   A bishop, named Ugenius, who witnessed the miracle, baptized the child, giving him the Irish name of Mulloc. These events are alleged to have taken place in the city of Hardbrecius.[2]   By Bishop Ugenius the boy was virtuously reared, and under his care learned to repeat the creed contained in the "Confessions of St Patrick,"[3] and the beautiful hymn attributed to that saint.   Fragments of this hymn, recited by the Irish peasantry, are not unworthy of quotation :

I.

" I bind to myself to-day—
The strong power of the invocation of the Trinity,

---

[1] Skene's Celt. Scot., ii. 203.   [2] Libell. de Ort., cap. xiv.
[3] Todd's Life of St Patrick, p. 390 ; Maclear's Conversion of the West—The Celts, p. 90.

The faith of the Trinity in Unity,
The Creator of the Elements.

II.

" I bind to myself to-day—
The power of the Incarnation of Christ, with that of
His Baptism ;
The power of the Crucifixion, with that of His Burial ;
The power of the Resurrection, with the Ascension ;
The power of the coming to the sentence of Judgment.

III.

" I bind to myself to-day—
The power of the love of seraphim,
In the obedience of angels,
In the hope of Resurrection unto reward,
In the prayers of the noble Fathers,
In the predictions of the Prophets,
In the teaching of apostles,
In the faith of confessors,
In the purity of holy virgins,
In the acts of righteous men.

IV.

" I bind to myself to-day—
The power of Heaven,
The light of the Sun,
The whiteness of Snow,
The force of Fire,
The flashing of Lightning,
The velocity of Wind,
The depth of the Sea,

The stability of the Earth,
The hardness of Rocks.

V.

" I bind to myself to-day—
The Power of God to guide me,
The Might of God to uphold me,
The Wisdom of God to teach me,
The Eye of God to watch over me,
The Ear of God to hear me,
The Word of God to give me speech,
The Hand of God to protect me,
The Way of God to prevent me,
The Shield of God to shelter me,
The Host of God to defend me,—
    Against the snares of demons,
    Against the temptations of vices,
    Against the lusts of nature,
    Against every man who meditates injury to me,—
      Whether far or near,
      With few or with many.

VI.

" I have set around me all these powers—
Against every hostile savage power
Directed against my body and my soul,
Against the incantations of false prophets,
Against the black laws of heathenism,
Against the false laws of heresy,
Against the deceits of idolatry,
Against the spells of women, and smiths, and Druids,
Against all knowledge which binds the soul of man.

VII.

" Christ, protect me to-day
Against poison, against burning,
Against drowning, against wound,
That I may receive abundant reward.

VIII.

" Christ with me, Christ before me,
Christ behind me, Christ within me,
Christ beneath me, Christ above me,
Christ on my right, Christ on my left,
Christ in the fort,
Christ in the chariot-seat,
Christ in the poop.

IX.

" Christ in the heart of every man who thinks of me,
Christ in the mouth of every man who speaks to me,
Christ in every eye that sees me,
Christ in every ear that hears me.

X.

" I bind to myself to-day—
The strong power of the invocation of the Trinity,
The faith of the Trinity in Unity,
The Creator of the Elements.

XI.

" Domini est salus,
Domini est salus,
Christi est salus,
Salus tua Domine sit semper nobiscum." [1]

---

[1] See Todd's St Patrick, the Apostle of Ireland ; James

This metrical prayer was called a " lorica," because, as a coat of mail protects from bodily hurt, its recitation was supposed to shield from spiritual peril.

After the death of Ugenius, Mulloc, who had previously been transferred to the care of a pious nobleman,[1] proceeded to Britain. The reason of his departure was, that, though a child in years, his wonder-working gifts caused him to be regarded with dislike. The manner of his voyage was miraculous. Embarking with his mother, his guardian, and two others, in a coracle hewn out of stone, he set sail during the night,[2]—a distorted version evidently of another legend, which relates how his body, in a stone coffin, floated on the Tweed.[3]   At the moment of sailing,

---

Clarence Morgan's spirited translation in the *Lyra Hibernica Sacra ;* and Dr Petric's Memoir of Tara, 1839.   Tradition affirms that St Patrick recited the above hymn when on his way to meet the Druidical fire-worshippers at Tara.

[1] Libell., cap. xv.   [2] *Ibid.,* cap. xix.

[3] Window in York Minster, see Archæol. Journ. York, iv. 281.

his psalter fell into the sea, and was immediately swallowed by a great fish, which, when the little company landed in safety on the Galwegian coast, ejected the volume uninjured.[1]

Arriving in Scotland, Mulloc proceeded to Dunkeld, in the Pictish country, which, according to the narrative, was the seat of Columba's episcopate. By Columba he was welcomed, and educated along with an Irish girl of royal extraction, named Bridgid. Numerous legends cluster round his life at Dunkeld. On one occasion some English clerics, jealous of the favour bestowed on the boy, killed a tame blackbird, a pet of the bishop, in the expectation that the blame would fall on Mulloc. But the bird's restoration to life, in answer to Mulloc's prayer, defeated the scheme.[2]

After a visit to Iona, where he discovered his two maternal uncles, he bade farewell to

---

[1] Window in York Minster, see Archæol. Journ. York, iv. 279.

[2] Libell., cap. xxi.

his mother, who had undertaken a pilgrimage to Rome, and proceeded to Lothian, and there took up his residence near the spot where the church of Childeschirche was afterwards built, and dedicated to his memory. This is identified with Channelkirk, a parish in the upper valley of the river Leader. There the Irish legends leave him.[1]

Extravagant and inaccurate as this account of Cuthberht's youth unquestionably is, it need not be rejected as wholly fabulous. The error respecting Columba, who is represented as alive about forty years subsequent to his death, may have arisen in this way. The Norse invasions rendered Iona insecure as the centre of the Columban Church; while the growing importance of Kells, in Ireland, overshadowed the parent establishment. When, therefore, the seat of civil government was fixed by Kenneth Macalpine at Dunkeld, the ecclesiastical see was likewise removed to that city, and a second

[1] Skene's Celt. Scot., ii. 204, 205.

Iona founded there, which was named in honour of Columba.[1]

In connection with Cuthberht's residence at Dunkeld other legends are narrated, which evidently refer to a later period of his life. By Bæda, in the metrical history, he is distinctly claimed as a native of Britain; but his warm sympathies with the Celtic Church would seem to argue a Celtic origin.[2] While, therefore, we may not, like the Bollandists,[3] pronounce the story of his boyhood to be wholly fabulous, the question of his birth and parentage will always remain undetermined.

[1] Reeves' Life of St Columba, pp. lxix.-lxxi. According to Usher, the Columba of Dunkeld and tutor of St Cuthberht was one personage (Hist. Eccles., Dunelm., p. 24); but this statement has no foundation in fact, and was probably framed to get rid of the anachronistic difficulty.

[2] Montalembert in his Monks of the West, and Reeves in his Notes on Wattenbach, pronounce for the Irish extraction of Cuthberht; Mabillon and Lanigan incline to the opinion that he was a native of the Lothians.

[3] Bolland, compiler of the *Acta Sanctorum*, was a Jesuit priest, a native of Antwerp. He composed the lives of the saints whose festivals fell in the months of January, February, and March. After his death in 1665, the work was continued by Papenbroeck and others, who, being of the same school, are termed Bollandists.

CHAPTER IV.

CUTHBERHT THE SHEPHERD.

" And oft the craggy cliff he loved to climb,
    When all in mist the world below was lost.
    What dreadful pleasure! there to stand sublime,
    Like shipwrecked mariner on desert coast,
    And view the enormous waste of vapour, tossed
    In billows, lengthening to the horizon round,
    Now scooped in gulfs, with mountains now embossed!
    And hear the voice of mirth and song rebound,
    Flocks, herds, and waterfalls along the hoar profound!"
                            —BEATTIE'S *Minstrel.*

HIS Saxon biographers agree in representing Cuthberht as a native of the Scottish Lowlands. The nameless monk of Lindisfarne pictures the young shepherd " watching the flocks of his master in the mountains;"[1] and several localities in the rich pastoral vale where Leader and Tweed mingle their waters claim the honour of his birthplace. In some rude hut on the

[1] Vita Anon. S. Cuthb.—Bæda, Oper. Min., p. 262.

slopes of Earlston or on the southern skirts
of the Lammermoor Hills the apostle of the
Lothians was probably born, and his infancy passed among scenes which afterwards impressed the seer of Ercildoune
and awoke the genius of Scott. Modern
writers have associated his birth with the
village of Wrangholm, which lay along the
base of a hilly ridge nearly facing Smail-
holm Tower. Of this hamlet every vestige
has disappeared.

The story of Cuthberht's youth reads,
says Montalembert, "like that of a little
Anglo-Saxon of our own day." Wherever
laughter was rife, and frolic or sports
abounded, there would Cuthberht be found.
In boyish games he was the ring-leader,
and his mirth-loving sunny temperament
made him a favourite. Bæda relates that
he delighted to be in the company of other
boys, and to join in their diversions.
Having a vigorous and active frame, he
excelled his playmates in running, wrest-
ling, jumping, and all bodily exercises. He

possessed also the thoroughly British quality of pluck, never acknowledging defeat, or abandoning a contest until the victory remained with him.

The story of his life, related by Bæda, begins with his eighth year. At this period he was committed to the care of a widow named Kenspid, whom he called mother, and treated with filial affection. Many curious legends, not less extravagant than those recorded by the Irish chroniclers, are told of his boyhood. Thus Bæda, on the authority of Bishop Trumwine, who claimed to have received the anecdote from Cuthberht's lips, narrates that as Cuthberht was one day playing with his companions, one of them burst into tears, exclaiming, " Why do you, Cuthberht, whom God has set apart to be a priest and bishop, waste your time in idle sport ? " The words made a deep impression on Cuthberht, and from that day he began to exhibit a gravity of demeanour beyond his years.[1]   When afflicted

[1] Bæda, Vit. Cuthb., cap. i.; Vit. Anon. Cuthb., i. 4.

with a disease of the knee-joint, which, contracting the sinews, threatened to render him lame, he was cured by a passing traveller. The prescription—a poultice of flour boiled in milk—was efficacious; and the sick youth entertained the belief that in the stranger "clothed in white garments, and honourable to look upon," and mounted on "a steed of incomparable beauty," he had beheld an angel sent to his relief.[1]

Another legend[2] records his marvellous power of prayer. "Towards the south," writes Bæda, "not far from the mouth of the river Tyne, there is a monastery which was inhabited by monks, but now by a noble company of virgins dedicated to Christ." From the description, Tyningham is evidently referred to; and the narrative proceeds to relate how some monks had rowed up the river to procure timber, when a sudden gale, blowing violently from the west, drove their boat down stream into the open sea. There the

---

[1] Bæda, Vit. Cuthb., cap. ii.   [2] *Ibid.*, cap. iii.

frail craft was tossed in the heavy surf "like a sea-bird on the wave," and destruction seemed imminent. From the shore the brethren of the monastery and a number of peasants from the adjoining hamlet watched the spectacle, unable to render assistance or avert a catastrophe. No feeling of compassion moved the semi-heathen rustics. "They have banished our ancient rites and customs," they exclaimed; "no one shall pray for them; may none be spared!" Then Cuthberht, who was present, knelt down, and as he prayed the tempest was lulled and the boat safely reached the shore.

In becoming a shepherd Cuthberht probably followed the family vocation. In the extensive pasturages which, as *folk-lands* or commons, were left to their use, the shepherds made their homes, living in the open air day and night. We can fancy the young apostle watching his flocks by day on the green slopes above the Leader, and, on the Eildon Hills, folding them at nightfall. In

his early wanderings he became familiar
with a region which, as a missionary, he
was afterwards to traverse. No marvel
that, roaming over the solitary moors and
through the wild forests which then covered
the land, strange fancies occupied his brain,
and that marvellous dreams disturbed his
slumber. It is in connection with his shepherd life that we grasp the first tangible
date in his career. The sunset had faded
into twilight, and the twilight deepened into
night, on the last day of August 651. Darkness, like a pall, swathed the hill-side, and,
wearied with their toils, the shepherds slept
peacefully. Cuthberht kept vigil alone,
when a vision passed before his eyes. A
beam of dazzling radiance shone suddenly
out of the black night, and in its midst
appeared a throng of angels bearing, as in a
globe of fire, a soul to heaven.[1] Rousing his
companions he explained what he had seen,

[1] Bæda, Vit. Cuthb., cap. iv.; Simon Dunelm. de
Eccles. Dunelm., cap. iii.; Vita Cuthb.—Bæda, Op.
Min., p. 262.

adding that in his opinion it betokened the death of a great saint or bishop. Next morning he learned that Aidan had died at Bamborough at the time of his vision.

In the deep impression which it produced, this event was the turning point of Cuthberht's life ; he considered that he had been specially called to enter into religion. To him the shepherd-life had ceased ; the care of his flocks was surrendered to another. Although Lindisfarne was probably at no great distance, and as a religious school was already famous, being associated with Aidan's ministry, Cuthberht turned his steps to Melrose. In this choice he may have been influenced by the reputation of Boisil, who was then prior,[1] and as a native of the district, he may have been familiar with some of the inmates.[2]

[1] Bæda, Vit. Cuthb., cap. vi.

[2] Respecting this incident there is some discrepancy in the accounts given by the different biographers of Cuthberht. The monk of Lindisfarne states that at the time of the vision Cuthberht was tending his flocks " in montibus juxta fluvium Leder" (cap. iii. 24) ; but we

An incident, which is chronicled by Bæda, occurred on his journey northward. Overtaken by night among the moors, he halted at a shepherd's hut to seek shelter and repose. It was Friday, and he was tired and hungry, for, desirous of observing the obligation of fasting, he had rejected the hospitality offered to him during the day. Having tied up his horse, and fed it with a handful of dry grass, he proceeded to his evening devotions. While he was praying, his steed, nibbling at the thatch of the roof, revealed a bundle wrapped up in a linen cloth; and Cuthberht, opening the package, found therein some bread and meat, on which he made a hearty repast.[1]

have preferred the authority of Bæda, who affirms that the time of the vision was some days before Cuthberht's entrance into Melrose.

[1] Bæda, Vit. Cuthb., cap. v.

CHAPTER V.

" The heights by great men reached and kept
Were not attained by sudden flight ;
But they, while their companions slept,
Were toiling upwards in the night."
—LONGFELLOW.

FEW Scottish abbeys are more famous
than Melrose ; and the romance of
history which is interwoven with its
name has formed the theme of more than
one chronicler and poet. But we have not
now to do with that monastery which at a
later date was reared with all the architec-
tural splendour characteristic of Norman
churches. The buildings of the Celtic
monks boasted neither carved roofs nor
pointed arches ; they were constructed of
timber, and thatched with wattle or moss.

On the banks of the Tweed, distant about a mile and a half from the foundation of David I., was built the abbey of Old Melrose. The name, Mael-ros or Mul-ross, signifying the "bare promontory," described its position. At the point where it stood the river makes an abrupt semi-circular sweep, in the form of a horseshoe, round a narrow spot of land which, projecting from the thick forest which covered the country, presented an open surface of green sward. On the peninsula thus formed the monastery stood, while a stone wall built across the narrowest part gave protection from sudden attack. In the centre of the enclosure, on a gentle eminence, the monks reared their wooden chapel, which communicated by an archway with the adjoining sacristy.

The ground-plan of the monastery was quadrangular; and besides the oratory, various other detached buildings were scattered over its surface, among them the abbot's house, the kitchen, the refectory,

E

and the cells set apart for the entertainment of strangers. Of a ruder description were the wattle huts which served as the cow-houses, granaries, and stables. In the centre of the enclosure are still to be seen the pond paved with flagstones, in which fish were kept for the use of the monks' table; and the "Lady" well, shadowed by an ash-tree, from which supplies of water were drawn.

The scene, familiar to the eyes of Eata, Boisil, and Cuthberht, has suffered little change. The forest, less dense than of yore, has receded from the river banks; but still bold and abrupt rise the red and white cliffs on the opposite shore, and still the deep green waters of Tweed sweep with musical murmur round the grassy holm.

When and by whom the abbey of Old Melrose was founded is a question which remains unsolved. Its existence was probably due to the influence of Aidan. Eata, who held office as abbot at the time when Cuthberht joined the community, was one of the twelve boys whom the Bishop of Holy Isle "received to be instructed in Christ."[1] Between the years 634 and 643 disciples of Aidan founded cells at Coldingham, Tyningham, and perhaps also at Abercorn; these maintained connection with Lindisfarne.[2]

When, after several days of travel, Cuthberht dismounted at the portal of Melrose, he gave his horse and his spear to an attendant. Boisil, the prior, who was standing near, remarked to Sigfrith, a brother monk, "Behold a servant of the Lord!" Eata, the abbot, seems to have been absent, as upon Boisil devolved the duty of welcoming the stranger. When Cuthberht had explained his desire to embrace a monastic life, the prior greeted him warmly. The youth (for his age at this time could not exceed sixteen years[3]) was hospitably en-

[1] "Unus de xii pueris Aidani quos, primo episcopatus sui tempore de natione Anglorum, erudiendos in Christo accepit" (Bæda, Hist. Eccles., iii. 26).

[2] Chalmers' Caledonia, i. 325.

[3] "Unfortunately Bede nowhere gives us Cudberct's

tertained for a few days, until the return
of Eata, by whom, on the recommendation
of Boisil, he was admitted into the brother-
hood, having first renounced the secular life
and taken the monastic vow.   He then
received the tonsure,[1] and entered upon his
vocation.

To the rules of the monastery Cuthberht
zealously conformed, observing even a
stricter discipline than his fellow-monks.
In study, in labour, in vigils, he excelled
them.   His robust frame, strengthened by
the hardy life he had led as a shepherd,
enabled him to support the austerities and

age.   He elsewhere calls him at this time a young man,
and says his life reached to old age.   Cudberct resigned
his bishopric in 686 and died in 687.   He could hardly
have been under sixty at that time, and it was probably
on his attaining that age that he withdrew from active
life.   This would place his birth in the year 626, and
make him twenty-five when he joined the monastery
at Mailros" (Skene's Celt. Scot., ii. 205).

[1] The tonsure of the Columban monks was from ear
to ear—not coronal, as with Roman clerics.   The fore
part of the head was left bare, the hair being permitted
to cover the back of the head only.

privations which were demanded by monastic rule. He was extremely temperate, avoiding stimulants. With respect to food he was less abstemious, his body requiring to be nourished, that he might be fit to endure the manual labour which formed a part of his daily occupation.

It may not be uninteresting to examine the nature and duties of that life to which Cuthberht had now devoted himself. As a dependent cell of Lindisfarne, the monastery of Melrose followed the discipline of the parent establishment, and, like it, looked to Hii for spiritual direction. The brethren regarded themselves as *Militia Christi*, and each member on enrolment became pledged ✳ to abjure the vanities of the world. The measure of obedience exacted from them was clearly defined "even to death." At the shortest notice they were ready to set forth on long journeys, and to brave the perils of flood and field, of wild beasts, and still more savage men. At home they were content to put their hand to any

labour that might be required of them.
Body and mind were both exercised—one
in outdoor toil, the other in diligent study.
Théy enjoyed goods in common. Personal
rights in property were disclaimed, according to Columba's rule : "Be naked, in imi-
tation of Christ, and in obedience to the
precepts of the Gospel." Almsgiving was
especially commended ; but the disciples of
Columba exercised discrimination in select-
ing their objects of charity, and while hospitality formed a marked feature in their
practice, itinerant begging was discouraged.
Celibacy was enforced, and humility stood
first in the rank of virtues.

The little society, or "family," was governed by the abbot, who was called "pater,"
or "sanctus pater." With respect to Melrose and other affiliated churches, the abbot
was subject to the superior authority of
the Abbot of Hii, by whom he was consecrated. Invested with supreme authority
in the convent, he could relax or intensify
discipline at will. According to ecclesias-

tical polity he ranked as a priest, being styled presbyter. As such he officiated at the altar, and pronounced absolution. All matters relating to the daily life, labours, and mission journeys of the monks were referred to him; when absent his duties devolved on a substitute appointed by himself. Among the lesser officials are mentioned the butler (*pincerna*) and baker (*pistor*). The scribe does not appear before the close of the seventh century; and to his functions of transcribing the records and rules of the monastery were afterwards added the duties of teacher and lecturer.

The older monks were called " seniors ; " those who, from bodily strength or previous occupation, were fitted for outdoor labours were termed " working brethren ; " the younger members, who were receiving instruction, were styled "juniors." At Hii and at the other foundations strangers were received, who, under the names of proselytes, penitents, and guests, sojourned for indefinite periods, or dwelt in the vicinity.

The size of the monasteries varied consider-
ably.   The smaller were built to contain
150 inmates.   This was the number of
monks in Iona.

> " Illustrious the soldiers who were in Hii,
>   Thrice fifty in monastic rule,
>   With their *curachs* across the sea,
>   And for rowing threescore men."

The larger establishments of St Asaph's in
Wales, and of Lismore and Clonard in Ireland, contained respectively 965, 800, and
3000 monks.

As seats of instruction the monasteries
were most useful, for many young men
repaired to them to be taught.   In some
monasteries fifty scholars were received,
and in others a larger number was accom-
modated.   In Ireland and Scotland these
scholars were regarded as inferior members
of the clerical order.   Subsequently they
seem to have occupied the position of cot-
tars simply, living in the immediate neighbourhood of the monastery, upon lands
which were set aside especially for their

support. They built their huts of turf and branches of trees, and lived principally upon grain or vegetables, which they cultivated for themselves.[1]

The duties of the monastic brethren were simple, consisting chiefly in preparing food and in manufacturing such implements or articles as were required for domestic use or field labour. Farming on a large scale, as afterwards practised by monks, was impossible to the Columban clergy. It is doubtful whether they were solely dependent on their own efforts, or were supported by the contributions of their converts. Probably they cultivated as much land as yielded a return in grain or vegetables, and reared sheep and cattle in sufficient numbers to supply themselves with food. In the community some could bake bread and brew ale, and they obtained fish from the river or fish-pool, which, with eggs and poultry, formed the staple of their ordinary diet. At the arrival of guests, fresh meat was

[1] Book of Deer, p. cxxxix.

added—beef or mutton. The general practice was to dine in the evening; but a
noonday repast was also permitted. In
this respect the rule of Columba was less
strict than that of Comgall, which guided
the Irish Church; it resembled the Benedictine formula, by which dinner was
appointed for twelve o'clock, with supper in
the evening. On Wednesdays and Fridays
a strict fast was observed. Lent was kept
rigorously.[1]

Each brother of the monastery was clad
thus: An under garment, called a tunic, of
a white material, was worn next the skin,
and over this was drawn the *cuculla* or
cowl. This consisted of two parts, a hood
or cape, and a body or skirt. The *cuculla*
was generally made of undyed woollen stuff
of a coarse texture, and retaining its natural
colour. In cold weather or when travelling, a warmer garment—*amphibalus*—of the
nature of a cloak, was worn. Out of doors
and at work the brethren wore sandals;

[1] Reeves' Adamnan, p. 351.

these were taken off when they sat at meals. They occupied separate cells, in which each bed was provided with a mattress and pillow; as they slept in their clothes coverlets were unneeded.

Daily service was performed in the chapel, to which the monks were summoned by a bell—those only who were engaged in the necessary duties being exempted from attendance. Sundays and Saints' days were distinguished by three peculiarities—absolute rest, the celebration of the Holy Eucharist, and diet of better quality. The Sabbath was held to commence at sunset on the preceding day, and its services, performed at stated intervals, included the Vespertinalis, Missa, Matutina, Prime, Tierce, Sext, and probably also None. In celebrating the Sacrament or Mystery of the Sacred Oblation, as it was termed, bread and wine and water, mixed in a chalice by the deacons, was used. The priest, standing before the altar, consecrated the elements. If several priests were present, one was invited to assist the officiating presbyter, and to break bread with him in token of equality. But if a bishop officiated, he broke bread alone, as a sign of his superior rank. The brethren then approached the altar and partook of the Eucharist.

Easter was the principal festival, the period between Easter-day and Whitsunday being known as *dies paschales.* Then, indulgences were more especially permitted; Christmas was attended with similar privileges. Lent, on the other hand, was observed strictly as a period of fasting and preparation for Easter-tide. Fasts were also prescribed for every Wednesday and Friday during the entire year.

When any infringement of discipline occurred, or any grave offence against the conventual regulations was committed, the guilty monk, on declaring his penitence, and on his knees promising amendment, was absolved by the abbot. Penances were frequently enjoined, of which some were severe and rigid.[1]

[1] Rev. R. W. Church's Life of St Anselm, p. 67,

In the training of every monk, the study of the Scriptures, especially the Psalms, formed an important part. Some slight knowledge of Latin and Greek might be acquired, sufficient for the transcription of monastic rules or other documents, but there is little evidence of scholarship or culture among the Columban clerics. The circumstances of their lives were unpropitious to the cultivation of learning, and in this respect they compare unfavourably with churchmen of a later age.

Such is a brief outline of the life and discipline which Cuthberht shared in the monastery of Melrose. How far this mode of life was beneficial to him, or profitable to others, it is difficult to determine. As pioneers of industry and art, the monks were certainly useful. They practised the healing art, though in a sufficiently rude manner, and possessed and imparted a considerable knowledge of agriculture.

The principles on which they regulated their lives were, in the main, excellent.

Self-discipline and self-control were the chief
objects sought; and to use the words of a
modern writer,[1] "In an age when there was
so much lawlessness, . . . they upheld
and exhibited the great and then almost
original idea that men needed to rule and
govern themselves; that they could do it,
and that no use of life was noble or perfect
without this ruling. . . . Rude as they
were, they were capable of nurturing noble
natures, single hearts, keen and powerful
intellects, glowing and unselfish affections."
The age was singularly superstitious, as
appears by the incredible legends recorded
by Bæda. The sign of the cross was used
to banish demons, and to avert pestilence,
and for such trivial purposes as to bless
a milk-pail, unlock a door, or to endow
a pebble on the beach with life-giving
powers. Their weaknesses were those of
their age, but the influence of their virtues
has long survived them, for, in the religious
earnestness of Scottish Lowlanders, may

[1] See Introduction to Dr Reeves' Adamnan.

even now be remarked the result of teaching in the remote past by the wandering disciples of Iona and Lindisfarne.

In 651, the year of Aidan's death, Bishop Aegelbyrht preached the Gospel to the West Saxons. Two years later the conversion of the Mercians was begun by Ceadda, better known as St Chad, a pupil of Aidan and Diuma,[1] a Scotic priest sent by Oswin of Northumbria. The efforts of these missionaries aroused the ire of Penda, the aged King of Mercia. The stubborn pagan was not disposed to yield without a struggle, and once more his armies, strengthened by the hordes of his Welsh allies, were let loose upon the northern kingdom. The flood of invasion rolled steadily northward; Deira was subjugated, and the peasants of Bernicia felt the wrath of the conqueror. Oswin at length sought to purchase peace by the

---

[1] According to Fordun, Diuma or Winna is identical with the Finan or Finian, who in 651 succeeded Aidan at Lindisfarne. He ruled till 660, when Colman was despatched from Hii to be his successor.

sacrifice of his treasury; but Penda sternly
refused terms, avowing his intention to
extirpate all who professed the Christian
faith. He drove the Northumbrian king
to the shore of the Forth, and took possession of Giudi, an insular fortress.[1] But
the fortune of war was changed. Rallying
his forces, Oswin by a nocturnal attack
routed his adversary. Penda and thirty
Welsh chieftains perished in the battle,
which, according to Bæda, took place at
the river Winwoed, that is, Avon in Linlithgowshire. The name Winwoed signifies
"battle-ford," and there near the village of
Manuel (the Manau of the continuator of
Nennius, who has also described the conflict), is a spot known as the "Fighting-
ford." By some writers Winmoor, near
Leeds, has been assigned as the locality of
the battle; but this is improbable, as nearly

---

[1] Bæda, Hist. Eccles., iii. 24. The fortress of Giudi
was built on an island in the middle of the Firth of Forth,
which may perhaps be identified with Inchkeith (Skene's
Celt. Scot., ii. 258, *note*).

all the authorities are agreed that it was fought in the level country near the shore of the Forth.[1]

The victory of Winwoed changed the aspect of affairs. Oswin recovered his kingdom; and with Penda's death systematic opposition to the spread of Christianity ceased. Peada, succeeding his father in Mercia, was converted and baptized by Diuma, who, in the following year, became first bishop of the Mercians. In fulfilment of a vow made before the battle of Winwoed, Oswin, in 656, founded and endowed, at Whitby, a nunnery, which was assigned to Hild. As abbess she was, in 680, succeeded by Elfleda, daughter of the founder. Oswin and Peada became firm allies, and in concert reared the Church of St Peter at Medehamstede, afterwards known as Peterborough.[2]

On the death of Adelwald of Deira, Oswin united that province with Bernicia, and thus became sole ruler of Northumbria.

[1] Skene's Celt. Scot., i. 256.
[2] Ann. of Engl., pp. 32, 33.

F

His sway was, in its power and extent, almost imperial. He not only, writes Bæda, "held nearly the same dominions as his predecessors," but he "subdued and made tributary the greater part of the nation of the Picts and Scots, who possessed the northern part of Britain."[1] Since the days of Eadwin no such glory had been reflected on the Northumbrian crown. The Britons of Strathclyde, and the Dalriadic Scots, were both under Oswin's rule; over southern Scotland his sceptre was supreme.

The pacification which followed the victory of Winwoed opened a way for mission work in Galloway and other parts of Scotland. In this way Cuthberht may have penetrated to the remote districts beyond the Forth; and his experience in Pictland, detailed in the chapter appended to the Irish biography, may, if not wholly fictitious, be referred to this period. On a hill near Doil (which Skene identifies with Dull, in Athole[2]), he established a hermitage. His

---

[1] Bæda, Hist. Eccles., ii. 5.   [2] Celt. Scot., ii. 206, 207.

reputation for sanctity was supported by
several miracles. At the Rock of Weem,
about a mile from Dull, a spring is shown,
which, according to the Irish chroniclers,
flowed from the cliff at his command.
Falsely charged with an illicit amour, Cuthberht abandoned the district and returned
to the Lothians.

Alchfrith, son of Oswin, who, as King of
Deira, was associated in the government
with his father, bestowed on the Abbot of
Melrose a portion of land on which to rear
a monastery. This was in the year 660.
The spot selected was Ripon; variously
styled by Bæda " Inrhipum " or " In Wrypum "—probably a corruption of the Latin
words *in ripam*, descriptive of its position.
The abbey was built on an eminence near
the confluence of the rivers Ure and Skell.
To this monastery, in 661, came, from Melrose, Eata and Cuthberht. The latter was
appointed *hospitaller*. His duties were to
provide strangers with food and lodging.
Each guest, on arriving, was received by

Cuthberht, and introduced by him to the abbot, who bestowed a kiss as an assurance of welcome. The visitor was then conducted to the oratory, and, after prayers, was lighted to the cell prepared for him. After having washed, he was provided with refreshment in the refectory. If the stranger arrived on an ordinary fast-day, the strict observance was, in his favour, dispensed with.

A legend is related in connection with Cuthberht's duties as hospitaller. Entering one winter morning into the guest's chamber, he found a stranger already there. Cuthberht fetched water and washed the stranger's hands and feet, and proffered refreshment, which was declined on the plea that he could not tarry, "as the home to which he was hastening lay at some distance." Cuthberht renewed his offer, and left the apartment to procure food. On his return he found the cell empty, while the fresh-fallen snow showed no trace of footsteps to reveal the way by which the stranger had departed. But on the table were three newly-baked wheaten loaves of unusual whiteness and excellence, a miraculous thank-offering which convinced Cuthberht that, unawares, he had been entertaining an angel.[1] Many a weary traveller benefited by the hospitality of the monks of Ripon. Among the peasants of Deira the benign influence of their teaching was felt ; and on the banks of the Ure[2] was chanted the hymn of Columba, which Aidan had brought with him from Iona, and taught to his pupils at Lindisfarne.

" The Father exalted ; ancient of days, unbegotten
  Without or beginning or origin : ever existing
  Is and shall be : to infinite ages of ages.
  With whom is Christ, sole begotten ; with whom, too, the Spirit

---

[1] No. 7 of the panels in the Cathedral of Carlisle portrays this incident.

[2] This hymn, called the *Altus Prosator*, is found in the *Liber Hymnorum*. The excellent version given in the *Lyra Hibernica Sacra* is here appended, with a few alterations by the editor, Dr Todd.

Co-eternal in Glory, in Godhead alike everlasting.
We preach not three Gods : one God we proclaim and
     one only—
Sowing our faith in Three Persons : eternally glorious.

" Creator is He of blest Angels; Archangels and Orders,
Principalities, Thrones; of powers and also of virtues
Lest goodness and majesty lodged in the Trinity
     might be inactive.
Boundless in functions of might, and in beauteousness
     endless
Thus manifesting itself; employed in proclaiming
Graces celestial and vast; in boundless expression.

" Down from the summit of Heaven; of order angelic,
Down from effulgence of brightness; from loveliness
     peerless,
Fell Lucifer, whom God had made, pride proving his
     downfall,
And with him the angels apostate, in like ruin mingled,
He of vain-glory the author; of obstinate envy;
Though steadfast remaining the rest; in dominion
     celestial.

" The Dragon most potent and foul: terrific and ancient,
Serpent of slimy deceit; excelling in wisdom
Every beast of the earth; of force full and fierceness
He with himself downward drew of bright stars the
     third part
Into the regions infernal; and dark prisons diverse
Erring deserters of light; headlong cast by the traitor.

" In foresight deep the Most High ; had poised the
    harmonious structure.
The heavens above the earth ; had founded the sea
    and the waters
Also the up-springing grasses, the shrubs, with their
    twining tendrils ;
The sun the moon and the stars ; the fire, and all
    things needful ;
Birds with fishes, and cattle ; beasts, and all living
    creatures.
Last He created primal man : ruler of all around him.

" The stars that heightened the ether ; made all by one
    act of Godhead—
Structure amazingly great — united with angels in
    praising
The Lord of the mass immense ; Architect great of
    the heavens,
Glorious their worship and meet : their praise ever-
    lasting
All these, with noble consent, thanks to their Maker
    rendered
In free and heaven-taught love ; not from endowment
    of nature.

" Both our first parents thus, tempted, assailed, and taken
The devil a second time falls ; with his satellites
    banded
Horror their aspect filled ; woful the sound of their
    flight
Well may frail man, too, fear, well may he sink in
    dismay,

Unable, with bodily vision; to look on such terrible
     things
There are the fallen ones bound; tied in their prison
     house fearful.

" He, too, their chief, in the midst, thus by the Lord is
     cast down,
While the wide space of the air, darkly and densely
     is filled
With the tumultuous crowd; satellites set in rebellion
Hid from man's sight lest he, pursue their example
     and crimes;
Neither encompassing wall nor screen, their iniquity
     hiding
While to all is proclaimed their sin; even the soul's
     fornication.

" Up from the wintry floods, the clouds their moisture
     carry,
Up from the threefold depths of the sea, from ocean
     regions,
To the climates of heaven above; in azure whirlwinds
Destined to render fruitful, crops and vineyards and
     orchards
Driven along by the winds; issuing forth from their
     treasures
Erupting still in their turns, the pools of the ocean.

" The tottering glory of tyrants; the passing and present
Mightiest kings of the world, set aside by God's judg-
     ment.

So the just doom of the giants ; to groan beneath waters
Great is the torment : the burning of fire and consump-
tion
Plunged in the swelling Charybdis; drowned in Cocytus
In Scylla o'erwhelmed ; by waves and by rocks dashed
in pieces.

" Ever the Lord drops down the waters; bound in the
clouds
Lest they should all break forth, at once their barriers
bursting,
And from their streams of fertility, gradually flowing
As from the wedders of Ruie : throughout the earth's
regions
Cold alternate and warm ; at different seasons
Rivers that never fail are constantly flowing.

" By the power divine of Great God, are constant
sustained
The globe of the earth ; and the circle which bounds
the abyss.
The strong hand of God the Omnipotent : ever support-
ing
On its firm column, the same as beams of a building ;
Promontories, also, and rocks ; on solid foundations
Firm, and immovably fixed : and strengthened their
bases.

" To no man seemeth it doubtful : Hell lies in lowest
places
Region of darkness and worms : haunt of dreadful
creatures

Where is consuming fire: blasting with flame consuming
Where are the groans of men : weeping and gnashing
    of teeth
Where is the terrible wail ever heard of ancient
    Gehenna ;
Where is the horrid consumption of thirst, and
    anguish of hunger.

" Below the earth, as we read, 'tis known there are
    dwellers
Often in prayer whose knee to the Lord is bent.
Impossible still it is to unroll the book written
Sealed with its seven seals : with warnings abounding
Which opened yet He hath : and so became victor
Fulfilling the glory prophetic, that waits on His
    advent.

" That paradise at the beginning was by the Lord
    planted
Read we in Genesis written : record most noble
From whose gushing fountain head four rivers are
    flowing
And in whose flowery midst is placed the Tree of
    Life,
Whose leaves bringeth health to the Gentiles, fail
    not for ever ;
Unspeakable are whose joys : and also abundant.

" Who hath ascended to Sinai—God's chosen mountain ?
Who its thunders hath heard, beyond measure resound-
    ing
With the clang of the trumpet terrific fearfully pealing ?

Who the lightnings hath seen, wild flashing around?
Who the lamps and the darts, the rocks rent and fall-
ing?
Who but Moses : the judge of the people of Israel?

" The day of the Lord King of Kings most righteous is
nigh:
A day of wrath and vengeance: of darkness and cloud:
A day of thunders astounding : awful and mighty :
A day of trouble and anguish : sadness and grief;
When shall be ended the passionate love of woman,
Ended the strife of man : and the last of this world.

" Trembling we all shall stand, at the Lord's judgment
seat.
Then an account shall we render of all our deeds
Beholding also our crimes : spread forth in our sight
As well as the book of conscience, laid open before us
Then shall break forth most bitter weeping and sobs—
The day for obedience gone : the call for life service
withdrawn.

" The trump of the great archangel, its wonders pro-
claiming
The strongest cloisters shall burst : wide open the
tombs shall stand,
Rent by the freezing cold that chills this earth of
ours,
Then bone shall gather to bone, and joint to joint
As meets the ethereal soul : with the body again,
Returning to tenant the mansion where erst it
dwelt.

" Christ, the most mighty Lord : from Heaven descending
Glorious the banner signed with the cross ; shall shine
Stricken the two chief lights : in the heaven o'er head,
The stars to the earth shall fall as fruit from the fig-tree.
Earth's compass shall be as the blast of a furnace
that burns.
Then shall the waning hosts hide themselves in the
caves of the mountains.

" High shall the chanted hymns swell; all ceaseless
resoundings
Sung by the thousands of angels in chorus rejoicing ;
Joined by the living ones four, whose eyes are un-
numbered ;
Also the elders—the twenty and four on thrones seated
All 'neath the feet of the Lamb of God, casting their
crowns,
Praising the Trinity ever in endless repeatings.

" Fiercely indignant the fire shall devour the opposers,
All who refuse to believe that Christ comes from the
Father.
But we upborne, shall fly forthwith to meet Him,
And with Him for ever shall be; among orders celestial.
Eternal to each the reward attained by deserving,
Thus to remain in His glory, for ever and ever." [1]

---

[1] This hymn is included in the *Liber Hymnorum.*
The translation in the text is by Dr Todd, with a few
alterations by the editor of *Lyra Hibernica Sacra.*

CHAPTER VI.

WILFRITH AND THE EASTER QUESTION.

" Not sedentary all : there are who roam,
  To scatter seeds of life on barbarous shores ;
  Or quit, with zealous step, their knee-worn floors
  To seek the general mart of Christendom ;
  Whence they, like richly-laden merchants, come
  To their beloved cells ? or shall we say
  That, like the Red-Cross knight, they urge their way,
  To lead, in memorable triumph, home
  Truth, their immortal Una ?"
                              —WORDSWORTH.

THE sojourn of Cuthberht at Ripon was of short duration, for, in the year following its foundation, the Columban monastery was broken up by the advent of another monastic body holding different tenets though following a similar rule. In the words of Bæda, " Eata, with Cuthberht and the rest of the brethren whom he had brought with him, was driven home, and the site of the monastery he had founded was given for a habitation to the monks.[1]

The cause of this sudden revolution was the return to England of Wilfrith, leader in that section of the Anglic Church which acknowledged the supremacy of Rome. King Alchfrith, who was warmly inclined to the Catholic doctrines, bestowed on Wilfrith and his adherents the monastery of thirty families at " In Wrypum," which he had recently granted to the Scotic ecclesiastics. The latter, preferring to retain their own canons, abandoned the newly-founded monastery, and returned to Lindisfarne and Melrose.

The return of Wilfrith in 661 marks the commencement of a struggle between the Scotic and Anglic Churches, which was obstinately maintained for nearly four years. In 664, having come to an issue on the Easter Question, their differences were, at the council of Whitby, referred to the arbitration of the Northumbrian king.   Each

[1] Bæda, Hist. Eccles., B., v. 8.

side was represented by specially chosen delegates ; and the struggle terminated, by Oswin's decision in favour of the Roman clergy.

The principal opponent of the Columban Church, whose talents and energy contributed largely to secure this triumph, was Wilfrith. Montalembert describes him as a man of ardent and energetic temperament, " incapable of fear or discouragement, and born to live on those heights which attract the thunderbolt, and rivet the gaze of the crowd."[1]

Wilfrith was born in Bernicia about 634. Descended from a noble family he was, in his fourteenth year, introduced at the Northumbrian court. By the queen, Eanfleda, he was kindly received, and she readily obtained the royal assent to his project of entering the religious life. One of Oswin's nobles, being afflicted with severe illness, had determined to retire from the court and pass the remainder of his days at

[1] Monks of the West, iv. 371.

Lindisfarne, then governed by its first great abbot, Aidan.   Wilfrith accompanied him thither, and remained there about four years.   A diligent student and insatiable reader, he possessed a quick intelligence and pleasing manners.   By the brethren, both young and old, he was greatly beloved.

From an early period Wilfrith had a strong leaning to the doctrines of Rome. At the age of seventeen, he obtained from his father, with the sanction of Abbot Finian, the successor of Aidan, permission to visit the city on which all his thoughts and desires were centred.   How far he was encouraged in this resolve by Queen Eanfleda we cannot determine ; but it is certain that she recommended him by letter to her cousin-german, Ercomberct, King of Kent,[1] who, in common with the southern Saxons, followed

[1] The appended genealogical table will show the relationship :

Ethelberht, King of Kent, *m.* Bertha.

Eadbald.

Ercomberct.

Ethelburga, *m.* Eadwin.

Eanfleda, *m.* Oswin.

the teaching of Augustine. At the court of Ercomberct, Wilfrith tarried for a whole year.

During his sojourn at the court of the Kentish monarch, Wilfrith formed the acquaintance of Honorius, Archbishop of Canterbury, and was, under his tuition, indoctrinated in the rules and practices of the Roman Church. He also became intimate with several distinguished laymen devoted to the service of the Church, and to the advancement of learning. Among these was Benedict Biscop, a Northumbrian noble, of whom some account has been given in the introductory chapter. In company with this zealous patron of art, Wilfrith, in the autumn of 653, commenced his journey to Rome. His biographer draws a beautiful picture of the youthful traveller, then only in his nineteenth year. "He was pleasant in address to all ; ready for every good work, with a face that, in its unclouded cheerfulness, betokened a happy mind."[1]

[1] Eddi, pp. 3, 4.

G

Passing through central France, Wilfrith arrived at the city of Lyons, where he became the guest of Archbishop Annemund,[1] brother of Dalfinus, Count of Lyons. With his bright face, frank speech, and quick perception, Wilfrith won the archbishop's heart, and was adopted by him as a son. He received costly gifts, and was offered the governorship of a province and the hand of Annemund's niece in marriage. Wilfrith declined the offers, and urged the object of his journey. Reluctantly acquiescing, the generous prelate dismissed him with his benediction, and a request that, on his return from Rome, he would revisit Lyons. Wilfrith made the required promise, and, attended by an escort which the archbishop had provided, continued his journey. Impatient to reach Rome, his companion, Benedict Biscop, had left him at Lyons, and gone forward alone.

At Rome, Wilfrith studied theology under Archdeacon Boniface. He made a special

---

[1] Early English Church History, p. 89.

study of ecclesiastical law and of the Paschal regulation, which was soon to occupy a prominent place in English polemics. In these pursuits two years passed, and then Wilfrith turned his face homewards, having first received the blessing of Pope Eugenius I.[1]

Wilfrith's promise to the metropolitan of Lyons was faithfully kept ; for on his return he took up his residence with him for three years. While he was the guest of the archbishop he received the Roman tonsure, and continued his studies under the direction of the most learned of the diocesan clergy. In 658 a tragical event terminated this happy visit. On a charge of disaffection, the archbishop was hurried to Chalons, and there, by the command of Queen Baldechildis and Ebröin, governor of Neustria and Burgundy, was condemned to death. Wilfrith accompanied his aged friend to the scaffold, and was eager to share his fate. " What could be better," exclaimed the noble youth, " than that we, who are as father

[1] Eddi, p. 5.

and son, should perish together!" And when the blow was struck which deprived his benefactor of life, Wilfrith stripped off his cloak and offered himself to the executioner. But one was enough for the sacrifice. The devotion of the handsome youth touched the hearts of the spectators, and when they understood that he was a "foreigner of the race of the Angles," they demanded that his life should be spared.

After attending to the obsequies of Archbishop Annemund, Wilfrith left the country and returned to Northumbria. At the court of Alchfrith he was honourably received. He had left it, a boy, with all the bright hopes and ardent enthusiasm of a youthful nature; he returned, a man, with trained intellect, matured judgment, and the enthusiasm of youth tempered by trial and danger. Montalembert writes of him thus: "To the irresistible attraction which from his earliest youth he exercised over all hearts, there was now joined the authority of a man who had travelled, studied, and

seen death and martyrdom close at hand !"[1]
Intellectually superior to any of his English
contemporaries, and trained in all the
scholarly lore and subtle disputations of
the Roman priesthood, Wilfrith was fully
conscious of his power.   In Rome, while he
associated only with his equals, he found
his level, and was humble ; but soon after
his return to England a change took place.
Intolerant of what he deemed the whimsical
views and antiquated doctrines of the Scotic
Church, he showed that he was not unin-
fected with the spirit of domination which
characterised the Roman clergy.   Withal
he had a keen sense of duty, and the work
which he set himself to do he ardently
laboured to accomplish.

King Alchfrith had early evinced a pre-
dilection for the Roman faith in which his
mother had been baptized, and it is therefore not surprising that he welcomed warmly
so distinguished a scion of the Church of
Rome, and besought him to remain in

[1] Monks of the West, iv. 145.

Deira to instruct his people. To his request Wilfrith acceded, and thus commenced
a friendship between the son of Oswin and
the zealous champion of Rome, which the
biographer of Wilfrith has compared to the
love of David and Jonathan.

Land was granted first at Stamford, near
York, for the erection of a monastery; but
the abandonment of Ripon by the Scotic
monks enabled Wilfrith there to establish
his abode.   As Abbot of Ripon, he commenced his rule in 661.   He was not yet in
priest's orders; but when Aegelbyrht, who
had relinquished his see at Dorchester,
visited the Northumbrian court, Alchfrith
besought him to ordain his friend and instructor.   Aegelbyrht readily complied with
the king's request, without so much as
consulting Colman, the Celtic Bishop of
Lindisfarne.   A strange revolution must
have been at work in Wilfrith's mind, which
led him thus to seek ordination at the
hands of a stranger, to the disparagement
of those by whom he had been reared.

The three years which followed Wilfrith's return were full of strife. Priests of the rival churches labouring in the same mission-field were continually coming into collision. Countenanced by King Alchfrith, and supported by the court, the Abbot of Ripon was eager to engage in controversy, and Colman, the Celtic bishop, was not slow to accept the challenge. The royal household even was divided against itself; for, while King Oswin clung to the rule of the monks of Lindisfarne, his queen Eanfleda and his son warmly upheld the Roman doctrine.

About Easter-tide 664, at the suggestion of Bishop Aegelbyrht, a conference was arranged. King Oswin was appointed to act as president, and champions on both sides were carefully selected. The leader of the Celtic faction was Colman, who, as Bishop of Lindisfarne, possessed weight and influence. With him appeared Ceadda, Bishop of Essex.[1] The Church of Rome

[1] Bæda, Hist. Eccles., iii. 22.

was represented by King Alchfrith, Aegel-
byrht, ex-Bishop of the West Saxons, Bishop
Tuda, James the deacon, the priests Agatho
and Romanus,—the latter chaplain to Queen
Eanfleda; also by the now redoubtable
Wilfrith, Abbot of Ripon.

The conference was summoned at Whitby,
then known, not by its Norse appellative,
but by the Saxon name Streoneshalch, the
"bay of the lighthouse." There, in the
double monastery of Hild, grand-niece of
Eadwin of Northumbria, was held that
council, upon whose decision the fate of the
Scotic Church in England was to be determined. Hild has been named in connection
with the monastery established by King
Oswald at Hartlepool, whence she was translated in 658 to occupy the post of Abbess
at Whitby. She and her followers were firm
adherents of the Columban rule. After her
death she was canonised, and, in common
with most of the Saxon saints, was credited
with miraculous gifts. Popular tradition
affirms that the ammonites which are found

in the jet-veined cliffs were serpents which she had transformed. Among the dependent cells of Whitby was Hackness, founded in 679. At a later period the monastery was plundered by Danish rovers. The abbot made his escape, and carried with him to Glastonbury the relics of the sainted abbess. With Whitby also are associated the names of Caedmon, who there laboured, and of John of Beverley, Bishop of Hexham, who was trained in its school. After the Conquest the convent was disused as a nunnery.

The question upon which the rival Churches had come to an issue, and which their delegates had met at Streoneshalch to discuss, was not new. Differing in minor points of discipline, the Celtic and Roman Churches were especially opposed in their mode of Easter celebration; and it was on this question that King Oswin was invited to give judgment. In the year 590 it had been a subject of dispute between the clergy of Gaul and Columbanus, the Celtic mis-

sionary, who, with twelve followers, founded
the monasteries of Luxueil and Fontaines
in the Vosges.   In 634, the year of Aidan's
settlement at Lindisfarne, Cummian, Abbot
of Durrow, in Ireland, addressed a letter to
Abbot Seghine of Iona, in which he reported that after careful examination he
had concluded to accept the Roman paschal
computation as correct.   This method,
was, on the recommendation of Pope
Honorius, adopted by the clergy in the
south of Ireland.   During the episcopate of
Finian, a Scot, named Ronan, who had been
educated in France or Italy, re-opened the
question ; but being warmly opposed by the
Abbot of Lindisfarne, whose influence was
at that time supreme, he could effect no
reform.   The attempt of Wilfrith and the
Romanists to enforce this change upon the
Northumbrian people produced a revival of
the old dispute.[1]   In our introductory
chapter we have briefly indicated, in connection with Bæda's criticism of Aidan,

[1] Skene's Celt. Scot., ii. 159-161, 164.

the outlines of this difficult and complicated
subject ; but fuller details are necessary.

On this point the Celtic and Roman
clergy were agreed—that Easter should be
celebrated only on Sunday; but by the
different Churches the festival was not held
contemporaneously. The Celtic Church
observed Easter in the week commencing
from the fourteenth day of the month ;
the Roman Church in that commencing
from the fifteenth. By the former calculation Easter Sunday did not always fall
on the Sunday after the Passover, but occasionally on the day of that Jewish feast.
This difference arose from the adoption by
each Church of a distinct mode of calculation.
The Romanists accurately averred that the
system which they followed was more correct than that adopted by the Celtic clergy.
The Roman computation was based on the
cycle of Anatolius, Bishop of Laodicea,
which fixed the recurrence of the new
and full moons at a lapse of nineteen years ;
while the cycle by which the Celtic monks

regulated their calculations gave a period
of twenty-four years. The Roman method
is that which with a slight modification is
followed now.

It is easy to understand that this discrepancy in their calculations caused a considerable difference in the period at which
the festival was celebrated by the two
Churches. Thus, if the full moon fell on
the 21st March, agreeably to the Roman,
or on the 20th according to the Celtic computation, the Sunday following that full
moon would be assigned as Easter by the
former method, but by the latter Easter
would fall to be celebrated on the Sunday
following the next full moon, or, in other
words, an entire month later. This want of
uniformity combined with the scandal of
occasionally holding the Christian festival
coincident with the Jewish, was a reproach
strongly urged by the Romanists against
the Celtic priesthood; it was also a powerful argument in favour of reform. In his
letter to Abbot Seghine, Cummian remarked

that, while " Egyptians, Grecians, Hebrews, Scythians, and all the world were agreed to celebrate Easter at a fixed time, the Celtic Church alone was disjoined by the interval of a whole month." Such is a brief outline of the question which chiefly occupied the attention, and engaged the skill of the disputants at the Council of Whitby.

King Oswin urged upon his hearers the benefit of uniformity. He said, "It behoves you who serve one God to observe the same rule of life; and as you all hope to gain the same kingdom of heaven, so you ought not to differ in the celebration of the Divine mysteries; but rather to inquire which is the truest tradition, that the same may be followed by all." After this exordium, Bishop Colman briefly referred to the position of the Celtic Church. His words were interpreted by Ceadda for behoof of his Saxon audience, "My usage," said he, "is that which I learned from my elders at Hii who sent me hither, and which we understand is traced to Saint John.

I dare not change it, and I have no mind to change it. We hold it as an inspired tradition, that the fourteenth moon being Sunday, is to be kept as Easter. Let our opponents state their opinion."

All eyes were turned on Aegelbyrht as the highest in rank on the Roman side, but the wary prelate remembering his imperfect acquaintance with the language, was too astute to risk a bad impression at the outset; he accordingly craved permission that Wilfrith might act as speaker on his behalf. "We both agree," he said, "with the other upholders of the Church's traditions, who are present; and Wilfrith can better express himself in the English tongue, which is native to him, than I can through an interpreter." The excuse was admitted, and from this time the discussion was conducted by Wilfrith and Colman alone. Addressing the assembly, Wilfrith commenced his speech by explaining the manner in which he had seen the Catholic Easter observed in Italy and France. It

was, he said, similarily celebrated in Africa,
Egypt, Greece, and Asia ; and wherever the
Church of Christ was spread abroad, " save
only by these "—pointing contemptuously to
Colman and his adherents—" and by their
associates, who, belonging to distant parts of
two remote islands, are foolishly endeavour-
ing to combat the world."

To this scornful language Colman rejoined, "I marvel you should call us foolish
who follow the rule of the apostle whom'
the Lord loved."

" Far be it from me," replied Wilfrith,
" to charge John with folly; for he observed
the precepts of the Jewish law, while the
Church was still Judaized, and the apostles
were unable at once to cast off all the
observances of the law which had been
instituted by God. . . . So John began
the celebration of Easter on the fourteenth
day of the first month in the evening, un-
concerned whether the same happened on
a Saturday or any other day. But when
Peter preached at Rome, being mindful

that our Lord arose from the dead on the
first day after the Sabbath, he understood
that Easter ought to be observed so as to
stay till the rising of the moon on the fourteenth day of the first moon in the evening,
according to the custom of the law, and
when that came, if the Lord's Day was the
next, he that evening began to keep Easter
as we do now.   But if the Lord's Day did
not fall next morning after the fourteenth
'moon, but on the sixteenth or seventeenth,
or any other moon till the twenty-first, he
waited for it, and on the Saturday before,
in the evening, began to observe this holy
solemnity.   Thus it came to pass that
Easter Sunday was only kept from the
fifteenth moon to the twenty-first.[1]   But ye,"
he added " agree neither with John nor with
Peter; neither with law nor with Gospel."
When Wilfrith had sat down, Colman
appealed to the paschal canon of Anatolius.
Wilfrith remarked that in making this
appeal he fell into error.   " What have you

[1] Bæda, Hist. Eccles., iii. 25.

to do with Anatolius," he asked, "since you do not observe his decrees? For he, following the rule of truth, appointed a revolution of nineteen years, which either you are ignorant of, or which, if you know, you nevertheless despise."[1]

When Colman urged that it was improbable that Columba and his successors, men whose sanctity was attested by miracles, should be in error, the reply of Wilfrith was conclusive. "Concerning your father Columba and his followers, whose sanctity you say you imitate, and whose precepts you remark have been confirmed by signs from heaven, I answer that when many on the day of judgment shall say to our Lord that in His name they prophesied and cast out devils, He will reply that He never knew them. But be it far from me that of your fathers I should so speak, as it is more just to believe what is good than what is evil of those whom we do not know. I do not deny that they were God's servants.

[1] Bæda, Hist. Eccles., iii. 25.

H

Nor do I think that their observance of Easter was prejudicial to them, so long as they knew not a more perfect rule; and I believe that if any catholic adviser had come among them, they would have followed his admonitions, even as they kept those commandments which they learned and knew."[1] Then in a solemn peroration he warned his opponents of the mortal sin they were committing in rejecting the decrees of the Apostolic Church, and preferring the rule of Columba to the authority of Peter, prince of the apostles.

Such is the substance, as recorded by Bæda, of Wilfrith's speech, which, otherwise cogent and powerful, is marred by contemptuous allusions to his early instructors. But ardent reformers are seldom considerate of the feelings of others, nor do they calculate upon what they lose by ignoring that charity which their Master pronounced to be more blessed than the other virtues.

[1] Bæda, Hist. Eccles., iii. 25.

Wilfrith greatly impressed his Saxon audience. No one present could refute his asser-
tions, or expose the weak points of his
argument. None were present to show that
in his reference to St Peter's observance of
Easter he had exceeded the bounds of historical truth; and that he had conveyed an
erroneous impression when he endeavoured
to persuade his hearers that the Roman
Church, on the question in dispute, had held
an authentic tradition. Rome had formerly
been in error on that very point, and had
altered her old paschal regulation, by which
the Easter festival fell to be celebrated on
the sixteenth day of the moon. But Wilfrith
profited by the comparative ignorance of his
adversaries. What they believed they could
not prove; while the appeal to the majesty
of the first apostle, with which their wily
opponent concluded his speech, weighed
with the superstitious king far more than
any other argument.

"Is it true, Colman," said King Oswin,
"that the words, that on him should be

built the Church, were spoken to Peter by our Lord?" "It is true," answered Colman. "Can you show any such power given to your Columba?" pursued the king. "None," was the honest answer. "You both agree," proceeded the king, "that upon Peter was bestowed power to found the Church, and that the keys of heaven were given in charge to him?" To this query Wilfrith and Colman signified their assent. "Then," said the king, "I say that Peter is door-keeper of heaven, and that I dare not oppose him, but in all things must submit to his authority, lest, when I reach the gates of the celestial city, they be closed against me."

The nobles and freemen present raised their hands to signify approval of the king's decision; and the council broke up.

Contented with the result, Ceadda returned to his East-Saxon diocese; but at the time he was the only notable convert to Wilfrith's eloquence. Bishop Aegelbyrht departed to France, there to convey to his fellow-countrymen tidings of the Roman triumph. On Wilfrith, the hero of the hour, abundant honours were bestowed. He was created Archbishop of York, in succession to Paulinus, who, thirty years before, had been expelled from that see.

To the decision of the king Colman submitted, but he peremptorily refused to acknowledge the authority of Rome, or to conform the usages of his Church with those of the Roman clergy. He preferred to relinquish his mission. We cannot withhold our admiration and sympathy as we behold him preparing to abandon the monastery over which he had ruled, and which he must have associated with hallowed memories.[1] From this trial he did not flinch. Taking with him some of the bones of Aidan, as memorials of the founder

---

[1] Bæda informs us, " that Colman, perceiving his doctrine was rejected and his sect despised, took with him such as were willing to follow him, and would not comply with the Catholic Easter and the coronal tonsure (for there was much controversy about that also), and went back into Scotia or Ireland to consult with his people what was to be done."—Hist. Eccles., iii. 25.

of Lindisfarne, he caused the remainder to be buried in the sacristy. We can imagine his progress on that sad journey along the Northumbrian coast, and over the rugged mountains and bleak moors of the Scottish Lowlands. All the Celtic monks, also thirty Northumbrians, who were members of the community, followed his fortunes. With him they went first to Hii, and there made report to the superior of the Columban Church. It was probably at this time, that Colman founded the Church of Fearn in Angus, dedicated to Aidan, and that of Tarbet in Easter Ross, which is associated with his own name.[1] Four years later, about 668, he proceeded to Ireland, and there, on the island of Innisboffin, established a monastery.[2] Harmony, however, did not prevail among his Celtic and Anglic adherents. The reason, as stated by Bæda, is not without interest to those who are acquainted with the nature of the Celt as

[1] Skene's Celt. Scot., ii. 167.
[2] Scot. Kal., pp. 303, 304.

he is still to be found in the Scottish Highlands or in south-western Ireland. " The
Irishmen," writes Bæda quaintly, " used to
leave the monastery when the harvest work
commenced, returning in winter to share,
with their English brethren, the fruit of
labours in which they had not participated."
The result of this disagreement was that
the Northumbrian monks withdrew to the
mainland, and, purchasing a small tract of
land in Mageo (Mayo), founded an independent house, of which Tuda, a Scot, was
the first abbot. Respecting the close of
Colman's career, not much is known. He
died about the year 676 in Scotia, that is,
Ireland, on the little island where he had
settled with those who accompanied him
from Lindisfarne.[1]

The decision promulgated by the council
at Whitby was very important; it marks
an epoch in the English Church. The connection with Rome and dependence on her
authority thus inaugurated, endured for

[1] Scot. Kal., pp. 303. 304.

nearly nine centuries. Improved culture and a higher civilising power were attained, while in view of the subsequent degradation of the Irish Church, the decree by which old things were swept away cannot be regretted. Yet it is impossible not to sympathise with the zealous and unselfish devotion of the Celtic monks, and to wish that their labours had obtained a better recompense. Bæda, a member of a rival Church, has pronounced their panegyric: "The place which they governed shows how frugal and self-denying they were. There were very few houses besides the church found at their departure; indeed, no more than were barely sufficient for their daily residence. They had also no money but cattle; for if they received any money from rich persons they immediately gave it to the poor; there being no need to gather money or provide houses for the entertainment of the great men of the world. . . . The king himself, when opportunity offered, came only with five or six thegns, and having per-

formed his devotions in the church, departed.
But if they happened to take a repast there,
they were satisfied with the plain and daily
food of the brethren, and required nothing
more. The priests and clerics went into
the villages with no other object but to
preach, baptize, visit the sick, and, in brief,
to take care of souls. So free were they
from the curse of worldly greed, that none
of them received lands and possessions for
building monasteries unless they were com-
pelled to do so by the temporal authorities;
which custom was for some time after observed in all the churches of the Northumbrians. For these reasons," adds Bæda,
" the religious habit was at that time held
in such esteem, that wheresoever monk or
cleric happened to come he was welcomed
by all as the servant of God; and if people
chanced to meet him on the way, they ran
to him, and bowing, were glad to be signed
by his hand or blessed by his mouth. Great
attention also was paid to their exhortations,
and on Sunday the people flocked eagerly

to the churches or monasteries to hear the Word of Life."[1]

The victory was duly estimated at Rome, as the connection between the Anglic and Roman Churches was further cemented, and the authority of Rome emphatically vindicated. Theodore, a monk of Tarsus, was in 669, at Canterbury, consecrated Primate of the English Church. King Oswin had two years previously despatched a priest named Wigheard to Rome, with the view of his being ordained archbishop, but his emissary died soon after his arrival at the papal court.[2] Wilfrith had reached the summit of his ambition, and his fame spread beyond the narrow limits of his native isle. His diocese was co-extensive with the dominions of his royal master, and his episcopal authority co-equal with the regal power. He had no difficulty in establishing his doctrines among the sluggish and superstitious Saxons, who cared little whether

---

[1] Bæda, Hist. Eccles., iii. 26.
[2] Ann. Eng., 8vo, 1876, p. 33.

the tenets of their religion were derived through Peter or Columba. But the inhabitants of the Western Highlands were beyond the influence of his rule, and remained faithful to the Church at Hii. It was no easy path that Wilfrith had to tread. From the hour of his elevation to the archbishopric, care and strife beset him. Thrice was he deprived of his honours and driven into exile; and the close of his life was embittered by the unpopularity which he had awakened through his unconciliating temper.

To both parties the Church of England owes a debt of gratitude—to the Celtic monks for sowing the seeds of Christianity at a time when the land was sunk in barbarism; and not less to Wilfrith and his followers, who, retaining what was good in the system they supplanted, introduced a higher culture and a sounder educational standard among the people, both lay and cleric.

CHAPTER VII.

CUTHBERHT, PRIOR OF MELROSE.

" Soldier of the Cross arise !
  Gird you with your armour bright ;
Mighty are your enemies—
  Hard the battle you must fight.

" 'Mid the homes of want and woe –
  Strangers to the living Word—
Let the Saviour's herald go,
  Let the voice of hope be heard."
                    —Rev. W. W. How.

WHEN the establishment at Ripon was broken up, Cuthberht accompanied Eata and his other fellow-monks on their return to Melrose. There he became the companion of Boisil, the aged prior, who did not, however, long survive. He died in 664. Kent and Essex had been desolated by a deadly pestilence styled in the old chronicles "the yellow plague." The contagion spread northward, and some time in 664 was communicated to the monks of Lindisfarne. Many of them perished, including the abbot and Bishop Tuda.[1] From Lindisfarne, crossing the Cheviots to the vale of Tweed, the pest appeared at Melrose, the infection, doubtless, being conveyed by visitors travelling from one monastery to the other. Cuthberht was attacked, and the monks for a whole night prayed that his life might be spared. Rousing himself by a vigorous effort, Cuthberht called for his sandals and staff, and rose from his sick-bed. This procedure, which on a feebler constitution might have resulted fatally, contributed to his recovery, for from that hour he regained strength. The effects of the illness, however, he never wholly surmounted. Boisil was the next victim. Three years previously he had predicted the time and manner of his death. He

---

[1] Raine's Life of St Cuthberht. Tuda had been appointed Bishop of the Northumbrians, in succession to Colman, but died before he had well entered on his official duties.

then prophetically assured Cuthberht that he would be ordained a bishop. Boisil regarded Cuthberht as the fittest person to succeed him in the office of prior; and when the pestilence seized him, knowing he had not long to live, he summoned his friend to receive his parting instructions. Together they studied the Gospel of St John, dividing it into seven portions, of which one was read daily. On the seventh morning, when the task was completed, Boisil expired. During the brief period he was able to impart to his *protegé* valuable and important council. Cuthberht's appointment to the priorate was unopposed.

Outside the monastery the epidemic continued to rage furiously, especially in the villages. Under the affliction many of the peasants relapsed into paganism, and, to the great grief of their instructors, "put faith in charms and amulets."[1] On foot and on horseback the new prior traversed the district, exhorting his flock to continue

[1] Bæda, Hist. Eccles., iv. 27; Vit. Cuthb., p. 9.

steadfast in the faith. In those days it was most difficult to get rid of an epidemic. The diet of the people, consisting principally of salted fish or meat, combined with the lack of cleanliness in their persons and dwellings, intensified the violence of the disorder. And so the mournful story was repeated, time after time, through the long centuries of the Middle Ages, until other "visitations," as these pestilential outbreaks were termed, induced the necessity of paying respect to the laws of health and of practising sanitary reform. How far Cuthberht succeeded in his efforts to arrest the progress of the epidemic is unrecorded, but his unselfish devotion is known to have favourably impressed the people.

The vale of Tweed and Ettrick has long been celebrated for its rich pastoral beauty. Describing the district, a modern writer remarks : "Agriculture has chosen its valleys for her favourite seat, and drainage and steam-power have turned sedgy marshes into farm and meadow. But to see the

Lowlands as they were in Cuthberht's day, we must sweep away meadow and farm again, and replace them by vast solitudes, dotted here and there with clusters of wooden hovels, and covered by boggy tracts, over which travellers rode spear in hand and eye kept cautiously about them." Such were the features of the region in which Cuthberht pursued his labours. His teaching was successful; for, while sagacious in estimating character, he possessed a cheerful manner and address, which rendered him everywhere a welcome and cherished visitor. Unlike Aidan, he was accompanied by no loyal interpreter, whose presence might protect him from insult, and secure him a hearing. But the apostle of the Lowlands possessed an important advantage over his fellow-monks: he was familiar with the topography of the country, for he had often led his flocks along the steep fells and over the heathy wastes of the Lammermoors; and he was, if not peasant-born, at least peasant-bred. Simple in his fare, and homely in his manners, he could converse with the people in their own rustic tongue and with the rich Northumbrian burr, which he had caught in his boyhood.

His pastoral visitations were not, however, confined to hamlets at Melrose; from the coast of Berwick to the shores of the Solway his face was familiar and his presence welcome. The memory of his mission-journeys lingers in Lowland tradition; it is preserved in the numerous churches raised in his honour and dedicated to his fame.

Visiting the monastery of Coludi or Coldingham, he there tarried some days at the solicitation of Ebba, the abbess. At Coludi, as elsewhere, he spent a portion of the night in vigil and prayer, and for this purpose went forth when the other brethren were asleep. A monk, who had observed his departure, quietly followed him. Cuthberht walked to the beach, and entering the sea till the water was up to his neck, began to chant the hymnal service. When

I

his vigil was ended, he waded ashore and knelt upon the sand.   There is a legend among the Northumbrian peasantry that two otters stole forth from their lair among the rocks, licked his half-frozen feet, and wiped them with their coats, thereby restoring warmth.[1]   This legend illustrates the ascetic side of monkish discipline.   Cuthberht in this respect followed the founder of his sect.   Of Columba we read that he only slept while his attendant, Diarmid, read three chapters of the "Beati," and that it was his habit to recite the "three fifties" (or Psalms) until daybreak, kneeling on the shore.   When he lay on the sand, he left upon it the impression of his ribs; for he dispensed with night clothing whether of linen or wool, and slumbered contentedly with his body in contact with the soil, and a stone for his pillow.[2]

From Coldingham Cuthberht proceeded

---

[1] Bæda, Vit. Cuthb., p. 10.

[2] Skene's Celt. Scot., ii. 505; App. Irish Life of St Columba.

to visit the Picts of Galloway. Setting sail with two of his brethren, he landed on the day after Christmas somewhere in the territory of the *Niduarii*, who inhabited the district which surrounded the estuary of the Nith. As soon as he and his companions had disembarked, a storm arose, which prevented their again putting to sea, while deep snow-drifts deterred them from penetrating inland. Thus the little band was detained several days, suffering from hunger and cold. Cuthberht's faith was strong, while his robust frame enabled him to sustain the miseries which depressed his feebler companions. He reminded them of the Israelites who were miraculously supported in the wilderness. Retiring to the base of a cliff to pray, he there found some pieces of dolphin's flesh, which appeared as if freshly cut and prepared for cooking. Their wants supplied, Cuthberht and his companions waited patiently till the tempest ceased; and on the fourth day they again launched their

bark.[1]   Tradition affirms that on the spot
where the Columban monks were thus preserved, a church was subsequently erected;
and in Kirkcudbright—the name of a Scottish town and stewartry—we have a memorial of the visit.[2]

On another occasion Cuthberht, with a
young companion, was travelling through a
wild and lonely district.   They had brought
no provisions, trusting to arrive at their
destination before night-fall; and at sunset
they reached the bank of a large river.
The shades of evening descended, and they
were yet far from any habitation, and knew
not where to obtain shelter and food.   Suddenly Cuthberht and his friend saw an
eagle soaring overhead, which, scared by
their approach, dropped a fish which it had
just caught and was bearing off.   The lad
who accompanied Cuthberht ran forward
and picked up the prize, rejoicing.   Cuthberht rebuked him, saying, "God hath fed
us by means of that bird; cut the fish in

[1] Bœda, Vit. Cuthb., p. 11.   [2] *Ibid.*, p. 12.

two, and give one to His handmaid, as her service deserves."[1]

During one of his journeys Cuthberht visited at Wrangholm the widow Kenspid, who had tended him in youth. While he was sojourning at her dwelling, a fire broke out which threatened to destroy the hamlet. At his prayer the conflagration was arrested, and, as in the case of Aidan at Bamborough, the village was preserved.[2]

The kind remembrance of his former protectress, who had been to him as a mother, and the friendships which he formed with Ebba, Hild, and other celebrated and pious women, are not consistent with the ascetic character assigned to Cuthberht by certain writers. It has been said that he had a strong dislike and contempt for women; and in proof of this, a red line is pointed out on the marble pavement of Durham Cathedral, beyond which he would permit no female to pass. Whatever the rules of his self-discipline might

---

[1] Bæda, Vit. Cuthb., p. 12.   [2] *Ibid.*, p. 14.

require when he withdrew to the seclusion
of Farne Island and adopted the life of an
anchorite, the record of Cuthberht's life
generally is at variance with this tradition.   And it is to be remarked that the
prohibition is mentioned by neither of his
biographers.   Possessed of a strong will,
he was withal humble and genial ; and his
disposition, if we read it aright, was untinged
by unreasonable asceticism.   The purity of
his life was above suspicion, and he enjoyed
the respect and affection of the many nuns
connected with the Northumbrian Church.
He was not deeply read, or a profound
scholar ; but he bore in his heart a warm
love to his fellow-men, and was ever ready
to aid the cause of religion and virtue.
A story which refers to a later period
of his life illustrates these kindly qualities.   Hildemer, one of Ecgfrith's courtiers,
who entertained Cuthberht in his house
when he passed on his diocesan visitations,
travelled to Melrose, where his bishop then
was, to beseech him to visit his sick wife,

or to send a priest to administer to her the holy eucharist. Cuthberht offered to proceed personally, and comforted the sorrowing husband by the assurance that on his return he would find his wife in restored health. The event confirmed the truth of his prediction; and Hildemer and his wife, now recovered from her illness, gratefully entertained their guest.[1]

The assertion as to Cuthberht's antipathy to women was probably invented by mediæval writers, who, claiming Cuthberht by conversion as a member of their Church, were desirous of representing him as cherishing the peculiar traits which characterised their own saints. True or false, the reputation thus attributed to him long survived in local tradition; and, in revenge for his alleged regulations concerning women, a cloth which he was said to have used in celebrating mass, and which was woven into the sacred standard borne victoriously by England on many a bloody field, was

[1] Bæda, Vit. Cuthb., p. 15.

burned by Calvin's sister, wife of the first Dean of Durham, after the Reformation.

" It is difficult for us," to quote the words of an eloquent modern writer, " to realise to ourselves what the pagan life which these early Celtic missionaries confronted really was—its hopeless corruption, its utter disregard of the sanctity of domestic ties, its injustice and selfishness, its violent and bloody character; and these characteristics could not be diminished in a people who had been partially Christianised, and had fallen back from it into heathenism. The monastic missionaries did not commence their work, as the earlier secular Church would have done, by arguing against their idolatry, superstition, and immorality, and preaching a purer faith; but they opposed to it the antagonistic characteristics and purer life of Christianity. They asked and obtained a settlement in some small and valueless island. There they settled down as a little Christian colony, living under a monastic rule requiring the abandonment of all that was attractive in life. They exhibited a life of purity, holiness, and self-denial. They exercised charity and benevolence, and they forced the respect of the surrounding pagans for a life the motives of which they could not comprehend, unless they resulted from principles higher than those this pagan religion afforded them; and having won their respect for their lives and their gratitude for their benevolence, these monastic missionaries went among them with the Word of God in their hands, and preached to them the doctrines and pure morality of the Word of Life."[1]

Of the precise character of that paganism which prevailed among the inhabitants of the Scottish Lowlands, and against which the efforts of the Celtic Church were directed, it is scarcely possible to present any full and accurate description. The accounts which survive in the writings of the earlier chroniclers are meagre and un-

[1] Skene's Celt. Scot., ii. 73, 74.

satisfactory, and, like the biographies of St
Patrick, St Columba, and others, they throw
very imperfect light on this dark period.
They were composed rather as panegyrics
to demonstrate the holy nature and miraculous powers of the founders of the Celtic
Church, than as sober narratives of historical
cal events. This much may be gathered.
Like the ancient Greeks and Romans, the
Picts and Scots worshipped the unknown
and invisible.   Their vivid fancy peopled
the lakes and groves, hills and rivers, with
mysterious divinities, whose anger was to
be deprecated and goodwill propitiated.   In
Ireland a survival of the ancient belief is
to be found among the peasantry ; and Scotland had her day of faith in fairies and
brownies, kelpies and hobgoblins.   Their
votaries were persuaded that these beings
could at will assume palpable forms and
associate with mankind. The legend runs
that the daughter of the King of Connaught,
coming early to a spring outside the village,
and there meeting St Patrick and his seven

companions, took them for the fountain's tutelary deities.

The Celtic missionaries had to do battle with many heathen practices, and especially with those connected with incantation. With them opposition took the form, not of argument or denunciation, but that of contrasting the purity and unselfish devotion of Christianity with the idolatry and immorality of pagan worship. The chief workers of unholy spells were the Druids, who by their magical arts claimed to appease the wrath of the gods, and induce them to grant prosperity. The life of St Patrick abounds with details of his controversies with this influential class, who filled important posts at courts, and were the counsellors of kings.[1]

By severe and continuous labour only could Cuthberht hope to counteract the degrading influences of evil teachers. He

---

[1] For an exhaustive account of the real nature and social position of the Druids, *see* Skene's Celt. Scot., ii. 110-119.

did not shrink from the contest, and was the first to preach the doctrines of Christianity, and to commend by his example a better life to the Galwegian mountaineers. But his term of office as Prior of Melrose was brief, for he was soon to be translated to another sphere.

Though not present at the Council of Whitby, Cuthberht and the community at Melrose were deeply interested in the issue. In quitting his island see, Colman recommended Eata as his successor; and doubtless in his journey through the Lowlands on his return to Hii, he visited Melrose. The brethren had not all accompanied Colman on his departure from Lindisfarne. Some remained, attached to their old home, and were willing to accept the proposed change rather than be driven into exile. Toward these Colman exercised a compassionate feeling, and on their account besought King Oswin to appoint as abbot one who had received his training at Holy Isle under the direction of Bishop Aidàn. The petition was granted; and Eata, without resigning the charge of Melrose, became Abbot of Lindisfarne, where, along with Cuthberht and others, he soon afterwards adopted the Roman rule. Cuthberht accompanied him from Melrose to Lindisfarne.[1]

[1] Bæda, Hist. Eccles., iii. 26.

CHAPTER VIII.

LINDISFARNE.

" Stern daughter of the voice of God,
O Duty ! if that name thou love,
Who art a light to guide, a rod
To check the erring, and reprove ;
Thou who art victory and law
When empty terrors overawe ;
From vain temptations dost set free,
And calm'st the weary strife of frail humanity !

.   .   .   .

" To humbler functions awful power !
I call thee : I myself commend
Unto thy guidance from this hour ;
Oh ! let my weakness have an end !
Give unto me, made lowly wise,
The spirit of self-sacrifice ;
The confidence of reason give ;
And in the light of truth thy bondman let me live ! "

ON his arrival at Lindisfarne, the new abbot proceeded to introduce the new rules determined by the Council of Whitby. In this work of reform, Eata was vigorously assisted by Cuthberht, whom he had appointed prior. Their task was no easy one. Though some of the brethren were disposed to submit to the Anglic Church, the majority favoured the old doctrine, and resisted innovation. Unlike Colman, however, their zeal did not induce them to abandon their home; they elected to remain and to adhere to the canons in which they had been trained. From the angry monks Eata and Cuthberht suffered personal insult. Cuthberht's attitude was most praiseworthy, his magnanimity being conspicuously displayed. Amidst reproach and contumely he never lost self-control, but would rise and go calmly out, and at next opportunity repeat his exhortations. In this manner he succeeded in inclining some of the brethren to adopt his views.

In discipline Cuthberht was strict. Whole nights were, in succession, passed in vigil and prayer, and when the brethren were asleep, he would steal forth to the rocky beach, and there wander about reciting psalms. At other times, in his cell, he would employ the hours of meditation in fashioning something useful with his hands.

In all that related to the internal regulation of the monastery, Cuthberht was a firm administrator. In the matter of dress he was especially exacting. The Celtic love of ornamentation infected even the monastic orders, but the Prior of Lindisfarne enjoined a simple costume of undyed wool. Opposed to ostentation, he himself wore garments "neither over rich nor slovenly." The rule thus enforced was generally adopted; "for," writes Bæda, "to this day it is not customary for any in that monastery to wear garments of costly material or gay colour, but to be content with the natural appearance of the wool." The material was woven into coarse frieze, capable of resisting moisture.

Every Sunday morning the Holy Communion was celebrated, when all joined in the sacred rite. Respecting this sacrament, the teaching of the Anglic Church was much in accordance with the modern practice of the Church of England. Gregory, the Anglo-Saxon apostle, designated the eucharist "a pledge of eternal life and a sacramental image." In Gregory's apprehension, therefore, communicants received, not the Saviour's substance, but a pledge and an image only. Bæda attributes to Christ's eucharistic presence a character merely spiritual, teaching that the sacramental bread had a mystical reference to the body of our blessed Lord, the wine to His blood. He further affirmed that Jesus gave to His disciples at the Last Supper the *figure* of His body and blood. In drawing a parallel between the Lord's Supper and the Passover, Bæda remarks, that Christ substituted for the flesh and blood of a lamb the sacrament of His own body and blood. " In the days of our venerable countryman," says one of our Bampton lecturers, "we are assured expressly the term ' sacrament ' meant a sacred sign."

From a passage in the " Homilies of Archbishop Ælfrid," we learn more precisely the teaching of the Anglic Church on

K

this subject: "Much is between the body Christ suffered in and the body that is hallowed to Housel, that is, the consecrated bread. The body, truly, that Christ suffered in was born of the flesh of Mary, with blood and bone, with skin and with sinews, and human limbs, with a reasonable living soul; and His ghostly body, which we do call the Housel, is gathered of many ears of corn, without blood and bone, without limb, without soul; and therefore nothing is to be understood therein bodily, but all is ghostly to be understood. And yet that lively bread is not bodily so notwithstanding—not the self-same body that Christ suffered in; nor that holy wine is the Saviour's blood which was shed for us, in bodily thing, but in ghostly understanding. Both be truly, that wine His blood, and that bread His body; as was the heavenly bread which we call manna, that fed forty years in the wilderness God's people; and the clear water which ran from the stone was then His blood, as Paul wrote, 'all our fathers drank of that ghostly stone, and that stone was Christ. They all ate the same ghostly meat, and drank the same ghostly drink.' And he said not bodily, but ghostly. And Christ was not yet born, nor His blood shed, when the people of Israel ate of that meat and drank of that stone. And the stone was not bodily Christ, though he so said. It was the same mystery in the old law, and then did ghostly signify Housel of our Saviour's body which we consecrate now." In the post-communion prayer we further remark the teaching of the Anglo-Saxon Church : "Grant that we may behold, face to face, and may enjoy truly and really in heaven, Him whom here we see enigmatically, and,—under another species,—Him on whom we feed sacramentally."

Cuthberht's labours were not confined to the monastery. Like Aidan, he wandered over the moorlands of Northumbria, teaching the people from house to house, and winning all hearts as he had done in the Lowlands of Scotland. So the years passed

quietly and uneventfully.   A new genera-
tion of instructors and missionaries rose up
under his guidance.   At length he chose an
eremitical life, which he had long contem-
plated.   In what year he did so, we cannot
precisely determine.   Skene places it in
670;[1] by other writers the year 676 is
named.   In either case it was prior to the
promotion of Abbot Eata, who in 678 became Bishop of Hexham.

Subsequent to the Council of Whitby,
the progress of the Anglic Church was
marked and important.   During the absence
of Wilfrith in France, when he was to be
consecrated bishop, Ceadda fulfilled his
duties at York.   On Wilfrith's return in
669, he was transferred to the see of Mercia.
From 669 to 678—a period of nine years—
Wilfrith administered the diocese of York.
His patron, King Oswin, having died in
670, was succeeded by Ecgfrith, his eldest
son.   Alchfrith, the pupil and friend of
Wilfrith, who had fought at Winwced, and,

[1] Celt. Scot., ii. 211.

in conjunction with his father, ruled the province of Deira, was, on account of his illegitimacy, passed over by the votes of the Northumbrian Witena, and thereupon withdrew to the Scottish Isles. At Iona he cultivated letters, and led a retired and simple life.[1] By his marriage with the sister of Peada, King of Mercia, he helped to establish Christianity in that kingdom.

In 673 the Synod of Hertford was held, at which was planned the partition of the Mercian diocese. The first-fruits of this council were the establishment of sees at Dunwich and Elmham, in East Anglia; in the following year Wilfrith founded a monastery at Hagulstad or Hestaldesheim, near the modern Hexham. In the previous year he had obtained from Ethelfreda, the consort of Ecgfrith, a grant of land for the purpose. The monastery was erected on a spot about twenty miles from Newcastle, where two branches of the river Tyne meet. Then followed, between 676 and 680, the

[1] Sharon Turner's Hist. Anglo-Saxons, i. 378.

foundation of the sees of Hereford, Lindisse or Lindsey (now Stow, in Lincolnshire), Worcester, and Leicester. Previous to 685 Wilfrith was deposed from his archbishopric, which was divided into the three lesser dioceses of Lindisfarne, Hexham, and York. Of these the first two were united under the charge of Bishop Eata, and the latter was conferred upon Bosa.

In adopting the life of an anchorite, Cuthberht followed the traditions of his Church. Seclusion was then held to be meritorious; and if it was an error, his apologists might plead the custom of the age. The disciple of Columba did not hold, with the poet, that

> " We need not bid for cloistered cell
>   Our neighbours and our work farewell.
>
>   .   .   .   .
>
>   The trivial round, the common task,
>   Would furnish all we ought to ask—
>   Room to deny ourselves, a road
>   To bring us daily nearer God."

Cuthberht was not of a temperament to shun a conflict or danger; he probably considered that in following a usage of the

Church he was maintaining his character for sanctity, and promoting the work of evangelisation. In the first instance, he withdrew to the mainland. Bidding his brethren an affectionate farewell, he crossed, staff in hand, the sandy isthmus, and sought at some distance inland a solitary abode.[1]

" On the southern slope," says Raine, " of a long ridge of hills, near the village of Howburn, is a natural cave, which has invariably been called St Cuthberht's Cave, or, in the words of the villagers, ' Cuddy's Cove,' and which, according to tradition, was at one period inhabited by the saint. Is there anything impossible in the supposition that this was the hermitage for which, in the first instance, Cuthberht quitted Lindisfarne ? Two things are certain, that the place of his retirement was

---

[1] A staff, evidently fashioned from the tooth of a narwhal, and which tradition assigns to St Cuthberht, was preserved in Durham as late as 1838 (*see* Raine's North Durham, p. 104).

not one of the adjacent islands; and that, wherever it was, it was at no great distance from the Church to which he belonged."

The cave thus mentioned was probably Cuthberht's hermitage. From the small station of Beal it is only a few miles distant, and it is therefore of easy access from Lindisfarne. The cave is now used by the farmers for a sheep-fold. Here Cuthberht took up his abode; and when the snow-flakes fell thickly and the wintry blast howled round his lonely rock, his voice might be heard reciting the liturgy or chanting the hymns of his Church.

One of the most beautiful hymns of this period was composed by Sedulius, an Irish theologian and poet; it comprises twenty-three stanzas. It is here presented in Canon M'Ilwaine's translation.

> " From the far rising of the sun
> To where his utmost course is run,
> Sing we the Christ of Virgin born,
> With kingly praise His name adorn.

"Though from eternity His sway,
 Our flesh He made His mean array;
 Redeeming thus from endless death
 The race that owed to Him its breath.

"The spotless Virgin's favoured womb
 Of grace divine becomes the home;
 And wonders, passing human thought,
 Unknown and secret, there are wrought.

"The maiden's bosom, pure abode,
 Becomes a temple meet for God;
 An earthly partner all unknown—
 THE WORD her offspring proves alone.

"The mother's thankful arms enfold
 The Babe whom Gabriel had foretold;
 Whom, though unborn, with prophet's eye
 The Baptist John could yet descry.

"In manger-shed, amidst the kine,
 All lowly lies the Babe Divine;
 Milk from a mother's breast is given
 To Him who feeds the birds of heaven.

"The heavenly choir their anthem raise—
 Angels unite their Lord to praise;
 While to the shepherds of the field
 The God Incarnate is revealed.

"Thou, hostile Herod, whence those fears?
 Is it that Christ on earth appears?

As though He grasped at earthly things
Who rules o'er all, the King of kings!

" The Eastern Magi, from afar,
Eager pursue the guiding star ;
Led by its beam, true light they seek,
And own their God with offerings meek.

" The matron crowd beholds, aghast,
To earth its infant offspring cast ;
Thus, through the tyrant's rage, doth rise
To Christ a spotless sacrifice.

" Where flows the river's cleansing flood
The Lamb of God all meekly stood,
By His obedience to atone
For our transgressions—not His own.

" His wondrous acts for Christ have won
His name—the Eternal Father's Son ;
Before His glance disease hath fled,
To life come forth th' awakened dead.

" The water owns a power Divine,
And, conscious, blushes into wine ;
Its very nature changed, displays
The power Divine that it obeys.

" Lo, the centurion comes to crave
Recovery for his dying slave ;
Such faith can pitying answer claim
And quench e'en fever's scorching flame.

" See Peter walk the swelling wave,
His Lord's right hand outstretched to save ;
The path, which nature's law denies,
To trusting faith still open lies.

" Four days within the noisome grave
Lay Lazarus.   He comes to save.
Rent by His word are Death's strong chains,
As life and light its prey regains.

" Deep crimson stains, a noxious flood,
Pollute the garment dyed with blood ;
A pleading suppliant draws nigh,
And straight the flowing stream is dry.

" A sufferer, palsied in each limb,
Pours forth his earnest prayer to Him ;
No pause ensues, no long delay—
Instant he bears his couch away.

" Now hath the traitor basely sold
His Master for the bargained gold ;
The kiss of peace he dares impart
While treason lurks within his heart.

" Vainly the JUST, the HOLY, pleads,
His back beneath the dread scourge bleeds ;
Nailed to the cross, on either hand,
The vilest of the robber band.

" The Sabbath dawns, and to the tomb,
With unguents rare, fond women come ;

To whom the angel voice is sped :
‘ Seek not the living ’midst the dead !’

“ Now raise we all the joyous strain,
    With sweet, triumphant, fond refrain ;
    The Christ hath conquered ! Death and Hell
    Redemption’s mighty victory swell !

“ Quenched is the dragon’s fiery zeal,
    Crushed is the lion ’neath His heel ;
    To heaven ascending, Thou hast trod
    The path of glory, Son of God.”

CHAPTER IX.

CUTHBERHT, THE HERMIT OF FARNE.

" O Jesu, teach me like Thyself to fly
This poisonous world, and all its charms defy.
Give me devotion which shall never tire,
Fix'd contemplation which my soul may fire;
A heavenly tincture in my whole discourse,
A fervent zeal which may my prayers enforce;
Of heavenly joys a sweet foretasting view,
That I on earth may only Heaven pursue."

—BISHOP KEN.

CUTHBERHT did not long remain in the quiet retreat that looked down upon the valley of the Till. Probably it did not offer the extreme solitude he desired. We find him, about the close of 676, constructing a fresh hermitage on one of the Farne group. The particular islet which he selected for his new abode is known as House Island; it is little more than two miles distant from the royal rock of Bamborough, and six from Lindisfarne.

Simeon of Durham describes the spot as unsuited for habitation, there being no fresh water, fruit, or trees in the vicinity. Trees and fruit could scarcely be expected to flourish on a bare, unsheltered rock ; but we read that Cuthberht contrived to raise some barley : his first crop was devoured by birds. To his brethren who visited him, he declared that if he could not support himself by the labour of his hands, he would return to the monastery. One of those legends, which in various forms are narrated of all the principal saints, tells us how Cuthberht remonstrated with the feathered plunderers, and how, at his rebuke, they ceased their depredations. In digging beneath the flooring of his hut, a spring was discovered, which supplied Cuthberht with fresh water.

Farne contains about five acres of grass land and eleven of rock. The soil is clay to a depth of six or eight feet. Basaltic rocks, rising abruptly to a height of eighty feet above the sea-level, fence the islet on the side facing Bamborough. The author of the " Life of St Bartholomew " describes the island as "a circle of solid rock, the top of which is thinly strewn over with a layer of barren soil. On its south side it is separated by a channel of about two miles in breadth from the shore; to the east and west a belt of rocks protect it from the fury of the sea; while on the north it is open to the whole force of the waves, in the midst of which it lies like the broken and defenceless hull of a shipwrecked vessel. Sometimes, when the tide rises higher than usual, and the wild storms of that rugged coast come to its aid, the waves make an inroad on the land, and the salt foam is blown over the whole island, wetting the shivering inhabitant to the skin, and penetrating the crevices of his habitation."

How awful and desolating is the power of the hurricane on those bleak and lonely isles, let the story of Grace Darling tell. In the early days of September 1838, a fearful storm burst on the coast of North-

umberland.   With sixty-three persons on
board, the " Forfarshire " steamer passed
through the Fairway (as the channel is
called which separates the islet from the
mainland), but owing to a leak in her
boilers, the vessel became unmanageable,
and at three o'clock in the morning struck
with tremendous force upon the Hawker
Rocks.   The piercing shrieks of the women
mingled with the screams of wild-fowl and
the roaring of the ocean.   The shouts of
the despairing crew were heard on the
Longstone Rock by the daughter of the
lighthouse-keeper, and at break of day the
miserable survivors were discerned clinging
to the rocks.   William Darling declared it
was impossible to venture out in so heavy
a sea, but his heroic daughter seized an
oar.   Her father followed her example, and
by their united exertions nine lives were
saved.   Grace Darling was twenty-two years
old when she rowed the frail boat over the
raging waves to the doomed ship.   Through
her golden deed her name is inscribed on

the roll of British heroines, and her memory associated with the rocks of Farne.

To see Farne as it was in the seventh century, we must sweep away the tall red lighthouse with its long reach of white-washed wall, and the three smaller houses which accommodate the lighthouse-keepers and their stores. The little chapel, though it is many hundred years old, was built long after Cuthberht's time, and Prior Castell's Tower is only a work of the fifteenth century.

The view from the island is interesting and extensive. To the east and north stretches the barren coast of Northumber-land; but distance lends enchantment to the view, softening the rugged outlines of the sand-hills, while golden furze and green waving bent lend their varied tints to mellow and adorn the landscape. South-ward lies the little fishing village of North Sunderland, and a low ridge of rocks crowned with the historic ruins of Dunstan-borough Castle. If tradition affirms truly, this was once a British stronghold, and would

L

have been a conspicuous feature in the
scene in Cuthberht's day; but no legend of
" Sir Guy the Seeker " would then invest it
with poetic interest, for the Norman fortress
was erected at a later date.   Far in the
distance, beyond the green slopes of Monk-
house, rise the rounded summits of the
Cheviot range; while, as the eye follows
the indentation of the coast, the proud
embattled pile of Bamborough comes into
view.   Beyond the grey mass of rock and
masonry are the Kyloe Hills, which look
down on the valley of the Till.   To the
south-east the long low isle of Lindisfarne
breaks the sea-line; and close to Farne lies
another island group—the Staples—separated by a narrow strait.   On the Longstone
Rock, in the midst of this dangerous archi-
pelago, was reared the lighthouse which
Grace Darling has rendered famous.

On the lonely islet of Farne, Cuthberht
built his hermitage.   Bæda describes it
thus: " This dwelling - place was nearly
circular, in measure from wall to wall

about four or five perches. The wall itself externally was higher than the stature of a man, but inwardly, by cutting the living rock, the pious inhabitant thereof made it much higher. . . . He constructed this wall not of hewn stone, nor of brick and mortar, but of unwrought stones and turf, which he dug out of the centre of the place." The biographer of Cuthberht further adds — " The dwelling-place was divided into two parts—an oratory and another dwelling suitable for common uses. He constructed the walls of both by digging round, or by cutting out much of the natural earth inside and outwardly; but the roof was formed of rough beams, thatched with straw." Cuthberht's hermitage probably resembled the primitive dwellings of the Irish anchorites, which were by them termed *Carcair*, or prison-cells. They were built of rough stone, with circular walls of great thickness and dome-shaped roofs.

Near the landing-place Cuthberht constructed a larger house for the accommoda-

tion of guests; but when the weather was
tempestuous, and the monks of Holy Isle
were unable to visit him, weeks would elapse
before his solitude was disturbed.   Then it
was that the recluse would feel all the lone-
liness of his situation.   From the cliffs he
would look over the stormy waters, and
say with the great founder of his sect—

" Delightful would it be to me . . .
 On the pinnacle of a rock,
 That 1 might often see
 The face of ocean;
 That I might see its heaving waves
 When they chant music to their Father
 Upon the world's course;
 That I might see the level sparkling sand;
 That I might hear the song of the wonderful birds,
 Source of happiness;
 That I might hear the thunder of the crowding waves
 Upon the rocks;
 That I might hear the roar by the side of the church
 Of the surrounding sea;
 That I might see its noble flocks
 Over the watery ocean;
 That I might see the sea-monsters,
 Greatest of all wonders;
 That I might see its ebb and flood
 In their career.

That contrition might come upon my heart;
That I might bewail my evils all,
Though it were difficult to compute them;
That I might bless the Lord
Who conserves all;
Heaven with its countless bright orders,
Land, strand, and flood;
At times kneeling to beloved heaven,
At times psalm-singing,
At times plucking dulse from the rocks,
At times fishing,
At times giving food to the poor,
At times in a *carcair*."

. . . . . .

Cut off from human intercourse, the solitary surrendered himself to contemplation and prayer. Hymns, such as the following, which he learned at Melrose, would be often upon his lips:

" Thou who all men dost relieve,
  Christ, in Thee I do believe;
  Come unto my aid, O Lord,
  While I labour for Thy word.

" Hasten to my help, I pray,
  Bear my burden every day;
  Of all mankind the maker Thou,
  Before Thy throne, our Judge, we bow.

"O Lord of lords, and King of kings!
To Thee all nature homage brings;
The angels, all alone in state,
In the celestial city wait.

"O God of gods, eternal Light!
O Lord, most high, most sweet, most bright;
O God of patience, past all thought;
O God, Thou teacher of the taught.

"O God, who hast made all that was,
Of past and present Thou the cause;
O Father, for Thy Son's dear sake,
Prepare the way that I shall take.

"And let Thy Holy Spirit guide
My soul through all my wandering wide.

"Christ, lover of the virgin choir;
Christ, man's Redeemer from hell-fire;
Christ, fount of wisdom, pure and clear;
Christ, in whose Word we hope and fear.

"Christ, breastplate in the hour of fight;
Christ, who has made the world and light.

"Christ, of the dead the living life;
Christ, of the living, strength in strife;
Christ, crowner of each conquering soul,
Who count'st it in the martyrs' roll.

"Christ, Saviour of the world so wide;
Christ on the cross at Passion-tide,

Christ into depths of hell descends,
Christ into heaven above ascends.

" Be glory to the Father given,
Exalted in the highest heaven ;
All honour to the only Son,
With God the Father ever one ;
And to the Spirit, holiest, blest,
Be equal power and praise addrest :
So be it until time is past,
And while eternity shall last."

Like St Benedict and St Francis of Assisi,
Cuthberht was distinguished for his humanity to the brute creation. His love of the
feathered tribes is still preserved in the
traditions of the Northumbrian peasantry.
Many quaint legends are told of St Cuthberht and the birds; on this subject Charles
Kingsley remarks, that we are not to
believe them; yet they convey lessons of
humanity which reach far beyond the in-
dividual existence of Cuthberht. He is
said for instance to have blessed the wild-
fowl of Farne, and bequeathed to them his
"peace." Another legend narrates how he
was wont to take up the young fledglings in

his bosom, while the parent birds followed him tamely. We have already seen how he reproved the sparrows who wasted his little crop; on another occasion he rebuked them for destroying the thatch of his guest-house. The sequel tells how they ceased their depredations, and brought him as a peace-offering a lump of lard, which Cuthberht kept to grease the shoes of his visitors.

The Farne Islands were the chosen resort in the breeding season of innumerable flocks of sea-birds. For the eider-ducks Cuthberht cherished a special regard, and with his successors in the hermitage these birds were favourites. "In this age of wanton destruction of wild birds," writes Charles Kingsley respecting the legends quoted above, "one is tempted to wish for the return of some such graceful and humane superstition which could keep down, at least in the name of mercy and humanity, the needless cruelty of man."

In tempestuous weather only did Cuthberht enjoy the solitude he so greatly desired, and which he had come to Farne to seek, for when the sea was calm he had numerous visitors not only from Lindisfarne, but from "the remotest parts of Britain,"[1] and his biographer assures us, no one who sought him in affliction, departed without consolation. Of his own merits he always entertained a modest opinion. Speaking with some of the brethren from Lindisfarne concerning the events of his own career, which Boisil had foretold, one alone he declared remained unfulfilled, which he hoped would never be accomplished. He alluded to the prediction that he would one day occupy the episcopal throne.

It is not to be marvelled at that Cuthberht, sharing the superstition of the age, should believe that demons hovered upon the island. When the wind howled round the desolate rocks, and the flying foam was hurled across the strand; when the thunder pealed, and the lightning flashed, and the

[1] Bæda, Vit. Cuthb., p. 22.

scream of the wild-fowl mingled with the
angry gusts, the solitary recluse might
easily persuade himself that evil spirits
haunted his island home. Near to House
Island are several long chasms or creeks,
known as the Wideopens or " Wedums,"
and the Noxes. To these narrow bounds
Cuthberht, when he arrived in Farne, con-
signed the spirits, whose shrieks continually
arose. Occasionally the demons seemed to
assume visible shape and form ; and we read
that Bartholomew, subsequently a hermit in
Farne, and his attendant monks used to see
them "clad in cowls and riding upon goats,
black in complexion, short in stature ; their
countenances most hideous ; their heads
long, and the whole band most horrible in
appearance. At first the sight of the
cross was sufficient to repel their attacks ;
but in the end the only protection was a
fence of straws, signed with the cross, and
fixed in the sands, around which the devils
galloped for a while and then retired, leaving
the brethren to enjoy victory and repose."

For eight years Cuthberht occupied the hermitage on Farne Island. The progress of the Anglic Church during that period has already been described. The diocese of York obtained further division. To the see of Hexham, Tunberct was appointed; Eata retained Lindisfarne, and Trumwine was consecrated Bishop of the Picts. His see was established at Abercorn in Linlithgowshire; it was the only episcopate of the Anglic Church north of the Cheviots. Probably about this time, Balthere or Baldred, an anchorite, founded the monastery of Tyningham on the river Tyne in the Lothians. Trumwine did not long retain his bishopric, for in the third year of his settlement, the turbulent Picts rebelled against the Northumbrian yoke. In 684, Bishop Trumwine was forced to abandon his see, and seek refuge with his patron, King Ecgfrith. Wilfrith—then in a sort of honourable exile—was absent on a mission to the West Saxons.

Once only do we read of Cuthberht

quitting his insular retreat. Elfleda, the princess nun, who had succeeded as abbess of Whitby the venerated Hild, desired an interview with him; and Coquet Isle, then occupied by a small monastic colony, was chosen as their place of meeting. After plying the pious hermit with questions relating to ordinary affairs, Elfleda revealed the real motive of her visit. How many years, she inquired, would her royal brother wield the sceptre of Northumbria. It was in no spirit of idle curiosity that the question was put. A crisis in political affairs was approaching. Already weakened by the long struggle with Mercia, and by years of foreign warfare, the Northumbrian kingdom was now menaced by an invasion of the Picts. Knowing her brother's restless ambition, and seeing on how insecure a basis his power rested, Elfleda wished to ascertain whether Cuthberht shared her apprehensions. The hermit of Farne at first attempted to evade the question, but the abbess pressed him to declare his senti-

ments. " Thou knowest," said she, "Ecgfrith
has neither son nor brother to be his successor, who then will inherit his kingdom ? "
Then Cuthberht replied, " Say not that
King Ecgfrith is without heirs, for he shall
have a successor whom thou shalt embrace
with the affection of a sister."   " But," proceeded Elfleda, " where may this successor
be found ? "   " Behold the sea," Cuthberht
rejoined, " how it abounds in isles, out of
one of these may God, if He will, provide a
ruler for Northumbria."   Then Elfleda
understood that he referred to Alchfrith,
the base-born son of Oswin, who was at
that time a voluntary exile in the Western
Isles.

Before the termination of the interview,
Elfleda strongly urged Cuthberht to accept
the bishopric which Ecgfrith was willing to
bestow upon him.   Cuthberht at first reso-
lutely declined the honour; but at last
moved by her entreaties, and remembering
the prediction of Boisil, he declared that if
he could as a bishop render the state better

service at such a crisis, he would no longer reject the dignity. He stipulated, however, that at the end of two years, he might be permitted to return to his hermitage, and finish his days in Farne. With this reluctant admission, the Abbess of Whitby was forced to be content.

On her return, Elfleda probably visited her royal brother, and communicated to him Cuthberht's acquiescence. Soon afterwards the hermit of Farne was summoned to take part in the synod of Twyford-on-Alne,[1] which was convened about the close of the same year. For some reason, not satisfactorily explained, Bishop Tunberct had been deposed. The Archbishop of Canterbury presided, and among the members present were King Ecgfrith and the fugitive Bishop Trumwine. Cuthberht did not appear, regretting probably his promise to Elfleda. On the suggestion of the king, and with the concurrence of the churchmen and laics assembled in council, Cuthberht

[1] Bæda, Hist. Eccles., iv. 28.

was unanimously elected to the vacant see
of Hexham.

Letters were at once despatched to ac-
quaint him with the honour which had
been done him. From all pleading, however, he turned away. Nothing could induce him to exchange his solitary cell in
Farne for the staff and mitre of a consecrated bishop. Probably he felt himself to
be, in comparison with Roman ecclesiastics, a rude and unlettered man, and did
not care to mingle in the intrigues of a
court, where his advice would necessarily
be in opposition to those who fostered the
vain-glory of an ambitious monarch. Not
till Ecgfrith in person visited Farne, and
joined his entreaties to those of Bishop
Trumwine and the powerful nobles and
ecclesiastics of his kingdom, was Cuthberht
induced to alter his decision. Proceeding
to Bamborough, the king, with his attendants, was thence rowed to the rocky islet.
To the royal pleading Cuthberht yielded at
last, but with reluctance. He stipulated

that he might be allowed to spend the time between his election and consecration in his hermitage. The request was granted; and Cuthberht, after a brief visit to the Northumbrian court, returned to Farne.[1] His consecration was fixed for the following Easter. Early in the winter of 684-5, Cuthberht visited at Melrose his former superior, Eata, and arranged with him an exchange of dioceses. Eata preferred that Cuthberht should have the superintendence of the monastery and see of Lindisfarne, and himself undertook the see of Hexham, to which Cuthberht had been appointed.

Easter of the year 685 fell on the 26th March. On that day the prediction uttered by Boisil twenty-one years before, was fulfilled, Cuthberht being consecrated in the minster of St Peter at York. Besides the Archbishop of Canterbury, six prelates assisted at the ceremonial, which the king attended in person. Before leaving York, Ecgfrith bestowed on Cuthberht a grant

---

[1] Bæda, Vit. Cuthb., p. 25.

of land extending " from the wall of St
Peter to the great gate westwards, and to
the city wall southwards," together with
the village of Crayke, the old city of Lugu-
balia or Carlisle, and a circuit of fifteen
miles around.[1]

[1] Bæda, Hist. Eccles., iv. 26.

CHAPTER X.

CUTHBERHT THE BISHOP.

"Temperance, proof
Against all trials; industry severe
And constant as the motion of the day;
Stern self-denial round him spread, with shade
That might be deemed forbidding, did not there
All generous feelings flourish and rejoice;
Forbearance, charity in deed and thought,
And resolution competent to take
Out of the bosom of simplicity
All that her holy customs recommend."
—WORDSWORTH, *Excursion*, b. vii.

LIKE many of his predecessors, Ecg-frith was the victim of unregulated ambition. War and conquest constantly occupied his thoughts. His rivalry with the King of Mercia cost much bloodshed; in a subsequent campaign in Ireland his arms were successful. But the inhabitants of the "plain of Bregh," which he cruelly ravaged, invoked the Divine vengeance on their oppressor. A few weeks after Cuthberht's consecration was planned an invasion of Pictland, then governed by a king named Bruide.[1] Remonstrances were unheeded. Deaf to the pleadings of his wisest counsellors, Ecgfrith departed on the fatal expedition. The presage of disaster cast over the land its gloomy shadow. Men remembered the imprecations of the oppressed Irish, and the burden of impending calamity was felt universally. In her sister's convent at Carlisle, Ecgfrith's consort, Eormenburh, awaited the result.

In connection with the expedition, fated to be in its issue so disastrous, occurred a remarkable incident. In common with Columba and other Celtic saints, Cuthberht was credited with the faculty of "the second sight." In the vision of Bishop Aidan, which decided his choice of the monastic profession, the gift had been exemplified. Once more, at a time of great national danger, the power of the seer descended upon him, and in a vision was

---

[1] Bæda, Hist. Eccles., iv. 26.

revealed to him the destruction of the Northumbrian host and its royal leader. It happened that shortly after the departure of the army, the newly-appointed bishop visited Carlisle. The townsfolk, with Paga, their reeve, sought to do honour to their bishop. On the afternoon of the 20th May, as Cuthberht was passing the town-wall on his way to the Roman fountain, he suddenly halted, leaning on his staff. To his attendants his countenance betrayed severe mental agitation. His eyes were bent upon the ground; but presently he turned his gaze to the sky, over which thick clouds were gathering, and groaning deeply, uttered in soliloquy: "Perchance even now the contest is decided." A priest among the bystanders urged him to explain his strange ejaculation.[1] Cuthberht answered, as if he were reluctant to reveal the nature of his vision. "Do you not see," said he, "how wonderfully the sky is changed and disturbed. Who can understand the judgments

[1] Bæda, Vit. Cuthb., p. 27; Anon. Vit., iv. 37.

of the Almighty?" Returning to the convent, he sought an interview with the queen. "Take heed," he said, "that you get into your chariot early on Monday morning, for it is not lawful to drive on the Sabbath.[1] Depart with speed to the royal city (York), for haply the king may be slain. To-morrow I have to visit a neighbouring monastery to consecrate a church. When the service is finished I will follow you."

On Sunday Cuthberht preached, exhorting his hearers to prepare themselves for tribulation. "I beseech you, my beloved," said the bishop, "to watch, remain steadfast in the faith, act manfully, and be comforted, that no temptation may find you unprepared."

The trouble was soon declared. On Monday a warrior, belonging to the army of the absent monarch, reached Carlisle. He bore evil tidings. Ecgfrith had crossed the Tay unopposed, his foes, by a feigned retreat, luring him into the fastnesses and heathy wilds of the Grampians. The North-

---

[1] Thorpe's Ancient Laws, p. 420.

umbrian host pursued eagerly, and at last
overtook them in a defile of Dunnichen.
There the Picts turned to bay, and a
desperate conflict ensued.   On the day,
and at the hour, that Cuthberht leaned sor-
rowfully upon his staff at Carlisle, Ecgfrith
fell in battle, and those of his army who
did not share his fate were made prisoners
or scattered.   The soldier who brought intelligence of the disaster had travelled day
and night, pausing not till he reached Carlisle.

In this conflict a decisive check was given
to the rule of the Northumbrian kings;
nor did they regain their supremacy for a
period of more than fifty years, till the
reign of Eadberct.   The scene of the conflict is still pointed out in the parish of
Dunnichen in Forfarshire.   At the foot of
a hill, formerly crowned by a fortified enclosure—(whence the name of the locality,
Dun Achan or " hill-fort of the valley," is
derived)—lies a marshy strip of land.   This
is designated the " mire " of Dunnichen, and

is preserved in the name of *Nechtansmere*, by which the battle was known to the ancient chroniclers. Near Rescobie on the shoulder of a hill, the remains of a fort are visible. The battle-field is under cultivation, but memorials of the struggle are occasionally discovered. On the East Mains or farm of Dunnichen, the ploughshare revealed a flat stone, on which was graved the rude outline of a warrior's head and shoulders. Cinerary urns of red clay, coarsely ornamented and filled with ashes, and mounds containing human bones, have also been dug up. These indications of a desperate conflict, attended with great loss of life, sufficiently identify the spot as the scene of the battle.

Bishop Trumwine, who had accompanied the invading army, was forced permanently to abandon his see of Abercorn. The family of monks were dispersed among various monasteries; the bishop established his own residence at Whitby.[1] There he survived

---

[1] Bæda, Hist. Eccles., iv. 26.

many years the battle of Nechtansmere. The body of King Ecgfrith, discovered on the fatal field, was at the request of Abbot Adamnan, who obtained it from the conquerors, conveyed to Iona, and there honourably interred.[1]

Overwhelmed by the loss of her husband, Queen Eormenburh found a retreat in her sister's convent at Carlisle. Affliction chastened her imperious nature; in the words of Wilfrith's biographer, she was transformed "from a she-wolf into a lamb."[2]

Alchfrith, illegitimate brother of the late king, was summoned from his retirement at Hii to succeed Ecgfrith.[3] Bæda styles him "a man most learned in Scripture, who nobly retrieved the ruined state of the kingdom, though within narrower bounds." Abundantly energetic, and trained in the school of affliction, Alchfrith was both a cultivator and patron of learning. With

[1] Reeves' Adamnan, 8vo, p. 232.
[2] Eddi, Life of Wilfrith, p. 24.
[3] Bæda, Vit. Cuthb., p. 24.

Adamnan he contracted a special intimacy; and the Abbot of Hii twice visited him after his succession. From him Benedict Biscop received countenance and help.

From the date of his nomination by the synod of Twyford, Cuthberht's tenure of office lasted about two years. It was long remembered by his flock. His faith in the unseen upheld him when calamity over-shadowed the land; while he endeared him-self to all by his humility and beneficence. His promotion to episcopal rank made no difference in his manner of life. According to the simple statement of his anony-mous biographer, "he continued to be the same man as he had been before."[1] "His discourses," writes Bæda, "were clear and plain; full of dignity and gentleness; he possessed the happy gift to know when to be silent, and when to speak; when to command, and when to reprove; when to distil the sweet balm of comfort, and when to rejoice with those who rejoiced. What

[1] Anon. Vit., v. 4.

he taught others he himself first did.[1]   He
was," adds the venerable historian, "in-
flamed with the fire of divine charity ; and to
give counsel and help to the weak, he considered equal to an act of prayer ; knowing
that He who said, 'Thou shalt love the
Lord thy God,' also said, 'Thou shalt love
thy neighbour as thyself.'"   We further
learn that he practically carried out the
precepts of his Master, to feed the hungry,
clothe the naked, and protect the widow
and orphan.

Cuthberht's episcopate of two years was
chiefly occupied in journeying to different
parts of his diocese.   Respecting his good
deeds are related many legends.   On one
occasion he visited the house of an earl
whose wife was believed to be dying.   The
nobleman warmly greeted him as he entered,
proffering hospitality ; but until Cuthberht
had refreshed himself by washing his hands
and feet, he forbore to mention his affliction.
He then told the bishop of his wife's illness,

[1] Bæda, Vit. Cuthb., p. 26.

desiring him to bless some water, that it might be sprinkled upon her. Cuthberht acquiesced, and from the moment the consecrated water touched the dying woman, her disease was arrested, and she began to recover. So quickly was she restored, the legend adds, that she was able to rise and in person present to the bishop the loving-cup, which constituted an important feature in Anglo-Saxon banquets.[1]

Among the nuns, who, after the battle of Dunnichen, sought refuge in the southern monasteries, was one, whose brother, Ethelwald, subsequently became Abbot of Melrose. For a year she had suffered from pains in the head and side which had impaired her health, but on Cuthberht anointing her with consecrated oil, the pain diminished, and she recovered.

In the course of his pastoral visits, Cuthberht was called upon to confront his old enemy—the pestilence, which, in the year following the battle of Dunnichen, deso-

[1] Bæda, Vit. Cuthb., p. 29.

lated Northumbria. The rustic population were in several instances forced to
abandon their homes, and many villages
were wholly deserted.[1]   With the courage
of his earlier years, Cuthberht went fear-
lessly among the sufferers, ministering to
the sick and dying, and bestowing consolation upon the survivors.   A legend relates,
how, like the Jewish prophet, he, by a kiss,
restored to life, a lad, the only son of his
mother, who was smitten by the pestilence.

Some time in the year 686, Cuthberht
made a second journey to Carlisle.   The
widowed consort of King Ecgfrith, who had
passed the period of her novitiate, was
about as a professed nun to assume the veil,
and Cuthberht desired to be present at the
ceremony.   During his visit, Cuthberht had
an interview with Hereberht, the hermit of
Derwentwater.   After some conversation
he said, "Speak now freely to me, brother
Hereberht, of any undertaking you have in
hand, for after we separate, we shall meet

[1] Bæda, Vit. Cuthb., p. 33 ; Anon. Vit., iv. 35.

no more in this life. I am certain the hour of my death is not distant." Greatly moved by these words, Hereberht threw himself at the feet of his aged friend, weeping and adjuring him not to leave him, but for the great love they bore to one another, to entreat the Almighty that He would suffer them, when their allotted time came, to die at the same time. Then Cuthberht, raising the hermit, reassured him, saying, "Rejoice, for God in His mercy has granted our request."[1] The sequel, Bæda is careful to note, proved the truth of the bishop's prophecy.

The hardships and labours of his earlier years, and the austerities which he practised in his hermitage on Farne Island, had undermined a constitution once robust. Before the expiry of the two years to which he had restricted his tenure of office, he resolved to resign his see, and return to his cell at Farne. He was already past middle age; for, assuming that at the time of his enter-

[1] Bæda, Vit. Cuthb., p. 28.

ing in 651 the monastery of Melrose he was in his seventeenth year, his age would be fifty-two. According to those writers who place his birth between the years 626 and 630, he would be still older. But he felt less the weight of years than the burden of increasing infirmities. His constitution had not recovered the effects of the pestilence which prostrated him in 664; and now, when the excitement which had sustained him through the troubled period that followed Ecgfrith's death was over, and the land was at peace, he felt that his pilgrimage was approaching its close. Before, however, taking the step he meditated, he made a farewell visitation through his diocese, exhorting his flock from house to house. At the request of Elfleda, he travelled to Whitby, where she had founded a church which she desired him to consecrate. Bæda relates the circumstances of this visit, which was distinguished by more than one exercise of miraculous powers.[1]

[1] Bæda, Vit. Cuthb., p. 34; Anon. Vit., iv. 39.

With this personal visitation terminated the episcopate of Cuthberht. If his term of office was not long, he well performed its duties. In the guest-hall of the noble and in the hut of the peasant his presence was welcomed. "In all things," writes the monk of Lindisfarne, "he observed the apostolic injunction that 'a bishop must be blameless as the steward of God; not self-willed, not soon angry, not given to wine, no striker, not given to filthy lucre; but a lover of hospitality, a lover of good men, sober, just, holy, temperate; holding fast the faithful word as he hath been taught, that he may be able by sound doctrine both to exhort and to convince the gainsayers.'"

CHAPTER XI.

REST.

" ' For ever with the Lord ! '
    Father, if 'tis Thy will,
The promise of that faithful word
    E'en here to me fulfil.

" So when my latest breath
    Shall rend the veil in twain,
By death I shall escape from death,
    And life eternal gain."

WITH the monks in Holy Isle, Cuthberht celebrated the Christmas of 686, and immediately thereafter withdrew to his much-loved solitude at Farne. Feeling that the labours of his active life had earned for him a peaceful retirement, he did not contemplate a return to the world. On the shore a number of the monks assembled to bid farewell to their revered pastor. Among them was an infirm old man. "Tell us, my lord bishop," said he, "when we may hope for your return." Cuthberht replied—"When you shall bring back my body."[1]

Notwithstanding his health, Cuthberht resumed the austere practice by which he had formerly regulated himself. From Bæda we learn the pleasing fact that he was not forgotten at Lindisfarne; by the brethren he was often visited. They desired to render assistance in case of sudden illness, and to receive the last advice of one renowned for his blameless life.

Of the last few weeks of Cuthberht's life, we possess a minute and graphic account in the 37th chapter of Bæda's prose biography. The narrative is given in the words of Herefrith, "the priest," eye-witness and actor in the scenes which he describes. He was then Abbot of Lindisfarne. To this office he appears to have been appointed on Cuthberht's retirement.

The months of January and February passed uneventfully. Cuthberht received

[1] Bæda, Vit. Cuthb., p. 37.

N

his visitors outside his cell, which, according to his wish, no one ventured to enter. Early on a Thursday morning in March, Herefrith, accompanied by a few of the brethren, visited the island. On approaching the hermitage, their greeting met with no response but a deep sigh. Then in feeble tones Cuthberht explained that during the night sudden illness had attacked him. He refused, however, to admit his visitors; and giving them his blessing, bade them return to Lindisfarne. "When the Lord shall have taken my spirit," said the solitary, "return, and bury me in this house near the oratory, towards the south, over against the eastern side of the holy cross which I there erected. At the north side of the same oratory is a stone coffin, hidden beneath turf, which Abbot Cudda gave me. Place my body therein, and swathe it in the fine linen you will find in the coffin."

Before leaving, Herefrith entreated his friend to allow some of the brethren to remain and minister to his need. The request was refused, and the little company reluctantly embarked. A violent storm prevented their return until five days had elapsed. When they again visited the island, they beheld a sad spectacle. Cuthberht had dragged himself from his cell into the guest-house, on the floor of which he lay prostrate. His face was ghastly and drawn with pain and fasting. After bathing his sores and causing him to partake of food and wine, Herefrith seated himself beside the dying bishop to receive his last instructions. Their conversation was brief. Cuthberht, who was hardly recovered from the delirium of fever, spoke of the persecutions he had undergone during the past five nights, but which were now over.[1] At Herefrith's entreaty he consented to receive some of the brethren as his attendants. At the same time he repeatedly averred that it

---

[1] Mediæval superstition pictured the grotesque and hideous fiends which disturbed the last hours of St Cuthberht. A window-painting in York Minster represents the dying bishop surrounded by winged demons of repulsive form and malicious aspect.

was revealed to him as the will of God, that in his last hours he should be left without human aid.   Among those who were selected to wait upon him were Bæda the elder, and Walstod, then himself an invalid.   Herefrith with the other brethren rowed back to Lindisfarne, but in a few days returned.   Then he communicated to Cuthberht the earnest request of the monks, that he would grant permission for his body to be buried in their monastery.   He at first refused, saying it was his wish to rest where he had for the Lord wrestled and overcome.   " Moreover," he added, " I think it better for you that I should here repose, on account of the fugitives and criminals who may flee to my tomb for refuge ; and when they have thus obtained an asylum (inasmuch as I have enjoyed the fame, humble though I am, of being a servant of Christ), you may think it necessary to intercede for such before the secular rulers, and so you may have trouble on my account."   As Herefrith and the other brethren still urged their request, Cuthberht at length said : " Since you seem wishful to overcome my scruples, and to carry my body to Lindisfarne, it seems to me that it will be the best plan to bury it in the inmost part of the church, so that you may be able to visit my tomb yourselves, and control the visits of others." They thanked him for this permission and counsel, and continued to pay him almost daily visits.

On the 19th of March, Herefrith and others carried the dying bishop into his little cell. Walstod went inside with him, " no one entering therein but himself." Six hours thus passed away, and about three in the afternoon, Herefrith found Cuthberht lying in a corner of the oratory, opposite the altar. He took his seat beside him, and begged him to send a farewell message to the brethren. Very faintly the voice which had stirred vast multitudes, uttered at intervals some words of counsel. " Let peace and Divine love," said the dying bishop, " ever be among you." Then he spoke of the duty of unanimity of agreement with other servants of Christ, and of hospitality to strangers. "Avoid all hypocrisy and self-righteousness," said he. The next injunction is remarkable, breathing the controversial spirit of the age : " Hold no communion with those who err from the unity of the Catholic faith, either by observing Easter out of its time, or by living perversely."[1] " Study diligently," pursued Cuthberht, "carefully observe the Catholic rules of the Fathers, and practise with earnest zeal those monastic regulations in which I have instructed you; for I know that in my lifetime some have despised me, but after my death it will be seen that my teaching should not be contemned."

Such is the account of the last words of Cuthberht, which Bæda asserts he received directly from Herefrith. The rest of the day passed tranquilly. When the hour of

---

[1] Bæda, Vit. Cuthb., p. 39. This injunction, if genuine, would intimate that the Scotic party had not been completely expelled from Northumbria.

nocturnal prayer was come, he received from Herefrith "the Communion of the Lord's body and blood to strengthen him for his departure;"[1] and, "with eyes gazing heavenward, and hands lifted high above his head,[2] he breathed his last in a sitting posture, passing away without a groan.[3] This event took place on the morning of Wednesday the 20th March 687.

On the day and at the hour when the spirit of Cuthberht took flight, his dear friend, the hermit-priest of Derwentwater, breathed his last. Hereberht had long been sick, and the story of his decease is thus beautifully celebrated by the poet Wordsworth:

"If thou, in the dear love of some one friend,
 Hast been so happy that thou know'st what thoughts
 Will sometimes, in the happiness of love,
 Make the heart sink, then wilt thou reverence
 This quiet spot; and, stranger, not unmoved,
 Wilt thou behold this shapeless heap of stones—
 The desolate ruins of St Herbert's cell.

---

[1] Bæda, De Mirac. S. Cuth., p. 36.
[2] Bæda, Vit. Cuthb., p. 39.
[3] *Idem*, Hist. Eccles., iv. 28.

Here stood his threshold ; here was spread the roof
That sheltered him, a self-secluded man,
After long exercises in social care
And offices humane, intent to adore
The Deity with undistracted mind,
And meditate on everlasting things
In utter solitude.   But he had left
A fellow-labourer, whom the good man loved
As his own soul ; and when, with eye upraised
To heaven, he knelt before the crucifix,
While o'er the lake the cataract of Lodore
Pealed to his orisons, and when he paced
Along the beach of this small isle, and thought
Of his companion, he would pray that both,
Now that their earthly duties were fulfilled,
Might die in the same moment.   Nor in vain
So prayed he, as our chronicles report.
Though here the hermit numbered his last day,
Far from St Cuthbert, his beloved friend,
These holy men both died in the same hour."

As soon as the spirit of Cuthberht had
passed away, Herefrith announced the
event to the brethren who accompanied
him.   By the flickering light of a couple of
torches was the sad intelligence telegraphed
to the monks of Lindisfarne.[1]   They were
chanting the first verse of the 60th Psalm,

[1] Bæda, Vit. Cuthb., p. 40.

"O God, Thou hast cast us off, Thou hast scattered us, Thou hast been displeased; O turn Thyself to us again!"

The mourners returned to Lindisfarne, conveying their sad burden.[1] A multitude of clerics and laics met them at the landing-place, and accompanied them, singing psalms, to the place of burial. The funeral obsequies were reverently performed. After being washed, the body was swathed in a fine linen sheet, well rubbed with wax, the gift of Abbess Varca. It was then clothed in the vestments which pertained to the episcopal rank, and in a stone coffin deposited at the right side of the altar in St Peter's Church. A kerchief enveloped the head, and on the breast were placed "offletes" or wafers, specially prepared for the eucharist.[2] Eleven years later, according to the monkish chroniclers, when Cuthberht's tomb was opened for the purpose of enshrining his remains, the body was found perfect and without decay.

[1] Bæda, Vit. Cuthb., p. 40.
[2] Eyre, Life of St Cuthberht, p. 81.

The coffin which enclosed Cuthberht's remains, Reginald of Durham describes as a
quadrangular chest of black oak, ornamented with delicate carvings, the lid being
flat and level. At the head and foot rings
were inserted, by which it was raised and
lowered. The chest was surrounded by an
outer case of timber, bound with hides and
secured by hasps and bands. A shrine, of
more elaborate workmanship, and richly
adorned with gold and gems, enclosed the
whole.[1]

When the Northmen began to make
descents on the English coasts, the costly
shrine was removed from one locality to
another to escape the invaders. At Chester-
le-Street it remained for a century. Ripon
for a time received it; but not until the
year 999 did the body of Cuthberht find
its final resting-place, within the walls of
Durham Cathedral. Behind the high altar
of that noble edifice the ashes of the pious

[1] Reg. Dunelm. Lib. de Admirandis B. Cuthberti,
cap. 43.

bishop have an honoured sepulchre. A plain blue marble slab in the chapel of the Nine Altars marks the place of sepulture. In 1827 the tomb was opened, and the dry bones of the saint were discovered swathed in the remnants of what had been a richly embroidered robe, figured with the portraits and names of saints, and adorned with a golden cross. These, with other relics of St Cuthberht, are preserved in the Cathedral Library.

Besides being the titular saint of the north of England, Cuthberht's memory was widely venerated in other parts of the kingdom. In Scotland numerous churches have been erected in his honour. Of these the most noted were Kirkcudbright, which preserved his name, Maxton, Ednam, Lorn in Argyleshire, and St Cuthberht's Church at Eadwinsburgh.[1] Through the presents of devotees, his shrine at Durham became wealthy. To quote the words of Montalembert: "The extreme veneration with which

[1] Kal. Scot. Saints, pp. 317-319.

the Saxon people surrounded the relics of St Cuthberht made this church (Durham) the best endowed in England. The humble anchorite, who had lived on his rock by the modest produce of his manual labour alone, thus created the richest benefice, after Toledo, in Christendom."[1] A banner of red velvet, with silk and gold embroidery, enclosing relics of the saint, was borne on many a battle-field. Richard III. took it with him to York in his progress through the kingdom; and as late as Flodden in 1514, it was carried in front of the English army. Its presence was believed to secure victory.[2] The fate of this interesting relic has already been described.

To Cuthberht's relics miraculous healing powers were ascribed. From all parts of

[1] Monks of the West, iv. 422.

[2] A legend runs that St Cuthberht appeared in a vision to King Alfred, and promised him victory over the Danes. Canute prayed at his shrine, and William the Conqueror respected the tomb of the Anglo-Saxon bishop. With the name of St Cuthberht are associated the battles of the Standard and Neville's Cross.

England invalids were conveyed to Lindisfarne, and there placed before his tomb.[1] Pilgrims annually visited Durham in large numbers on the 2d March, which was celebrated as his festival.

In these pages we have dwelt more upon Cuthberht the man than upon Cuthberht the saint; more upon his human, lovable qualities than on his miraculous powers. His pure, unspotted life, native benevolence, and unswerving zeal, won for his memory a respect which has never perished; while the miracles ascribed to him in the superstitious spirit of the age are, as idle inventions, forgotten or despised. It is always a difficult matter to draw the line between fact and fiction; but even among much that is necessarily rejected as absurd or impossible, it is not hard to trace the outlines of a noble nature, worthy of being quoted as a pattern in all time and in every land.

The supernatural element which so largely predominates in the biographies of Bæda

[1] Bæda, Vit. Cuthb., pp. 41, 44, 45.

and Reginald of Durham, is easily accounted
for.   The credulity of the age demanded
not merely a faithful pastor, but a wonder-
working saint; and the Bishop of Lindisfarne was the only one who could with pro-
priety be selected.   Raine on this subject
remarks: "Aidan, the first bishop, held
erroneous notions with respect to the observance of Easter; Finian was still more
heterodox; and Colman defended the custom of his predecessors.   Tuda, the next
bishop, died before he had an opportunity
of enriching a future legend; and any
miracle which might have been performed
by Eata, his successor, would have been
equally claimed by the see of Hexham." [1]
Cuthberht, accordingly, was the first bishop
on whom the dignity of patron saint could
fairly be conferred.   On the vexed questions
of Easter celebration and clerical tonsure,
he was at one with the Church of Rome,
while his pure and simple life eminently
fitted him for being accounted the apostle

[1] Raine's North Durham, p. 62.

and patron of the Northumbrian Church. Without, therefore, reposing credit in the fantastic legends of his enthusiastic biographers, we may in Cuthberht behold one who was adorned with the spirit, and trod in the footsteps of the early apostles.

After the death of Cuthberht, Wilfrith was, in the see of Lindisfarne, appointed his successor. His tenure of office was short; for about a year later we find Eadberct acting as bishop.[1] The intolerance of Wilfrith towards those who differed from him in doctrine alienated the affection and support of his royal patron; and five years later he was removed from the diocese of York. He appealed to Rome against Alchfrith's decision; but although the papal court decided in his favour the king remained firm, and he had to content himself with only a portion of his diocese. During the remaining years of his career, he governed the monasteries of Ripon and Hexham. At the latter place he began to erect

[1] Bæda, Vit. Cuthb., p. 40.

a church dedicated to the Virgin; he did not survive to see its completion. He died in 709, and was buried near the high altar in the church of St Peter at Ripon. The monastery which he had there founded, was subsequently destroyed by the Danes; but after the conquest, Archbishop Aeldred rebuilt and endowed it. A narrow archway called St Wilfrith's needle is still pointed out in the chapel.

Wilfrith was succeeded in the diocese of Hagulstad or Hexham by Acca, who distinguished himself by his zeal in preserving relics of the saints, and collecting materials for a library. Acca was a pupil of Bishop Bosa of York, and had accompanied Wilfrith in his wanderings and exile.

In 688, Adamnan, Abbot of Hii, who had repaired and beautified that ancient monastery, visited the court of Alchfrith, and had an interview with Abbot Ceolfrid at Jarrow. Through the instruction of this able priest, the friend of Biscop, the Columban abbot was converted to the

Roman faith. On his return he endeavoured to introduce among the monks of Iona the new doctrines, and especially the regulation respecting the celebration of Easter. The innovations were unfavourably received by the Scotic monks, but at the synod of Tara, in 697, the Irish clergy gave their submission. In 706, while Dunchad was abbot, Ecgbert, a Saxon priest, succeeded in converting a portion of the community at Hii. The remainder, who still continued obstinate in their opposition, were by a decree of Naiton, King of the Northern Picts — a convert of Ceolfrid—deprived of their offices. Thus terminated the supremacy of Iona over the Columban Churches.

About ten years later an Anglic see was established at Whithern in Galloway; in 731, Picthelm was consecrated bishop. The monastery was built on a peninsula jutting out into the sea, which, like Lindisfarne, became at high tide an island. Here in 397, Ninian had built a chapel of white stone, known as *Candida Casa*, the white

o

house.   The Church at Whithern continued
to flourish under a long line of Anglic
bishops, until the power of the northern
kingdoms began to wane, and the natives
asserting their independence banished their
instructors.   But the fame of the establishment did not diminish.   The remains of St
Ninian were interred in the monastery, and
until the year 1581, when an Act of Par-
liament condemned the practice, pilgrims
flocked to his shrine.[1]

Bæda does not bring down his history
further than the close of the year 731 ; but
from other sources we gather the principal
ecclesiastical events of the period which
succeeded the expulsion from Iona of the
Columban monks.   Up to Ecgbert's death
in 729, a strong party remained in the
monastery who strictly opposed the Roman
innovations, refusing to adopt the coronal
tonsure.   This opposition continued for
forty years later.   Then followed the period
of the Danish invasions.   In 806, the

[1] Dawson's Statist. Account of Scot., p. 1068.

Abbot of Hii, together with his "family," numbering sixty-eight persons, were cruelly slaughtered; and the timber fabric of the monastery broken up and levelled. The seat of the Columban order was now removed to Kells in Meath. The stone coffin containing the remains of Columba was disinterred, and enshrined in the Church of St Patrick on the shores of Strangford Loch. In 818, the establishment of Iona was revived, the new abbot presenting to his brethren the relics of their patron saint. The new monastery was constructed of stone, and the costly shrine was carefully concealed by a curtain of masonry, lest it should tempt the cupidity of northern rovers. A monk named Blethnac was put to death for refusing to reveal the shrine to a band of pirates. About the middle of the ninth century, King Kenneth Macalpine restored to his dominions the church of St Columba. Dunkeld was selected as the central seat of the new establishment. The bishopric was subsequently transferred to Abernethy, the

old Pictish capital, near which a round
tower still exists, which may have been
somehow associated with the Irish clergy,
who assisted in reconstructing the Columban Church.

In Ireland, and at a later period in Scotland, the expulsion of the Columban clergy
was followed by the appearance of an
irregular sect of clerics, historically known
as the Culdees.   Into the vexed question of
their origin we will not enter; it is clear
that their existence was a revival of the old
eremitical life, without that isolation which
was its principal feature.   Associating in
communities, they adopted a dress and discipline closely resembling that of the Columban clergy ; and like the monks of Iona
were characterised by a fierce opposition to
Roman doctrine.   But not until the days
of Wycliffe did a reformer arise to protest
against the assumption and superstition of
the Popedom, and lead back the Anglic
Church into the old paths.

APPENDIX.

I.

BISHOPS OF LINDISFARNE.

	A.D.
Aidan,	635
Finian,	651
Colman,	661
Tuda,	664
Eata,	678
Cuthberht,	685
Wilfrith,	687
Eadberct,	688

II.

KINGS OF NORTHUMBRIA.

	A.D.
Æthelfrith,	593
Eadwin,	617
Eanfrith (in Bernicia), Osric (in Deira),	633

	A.D.
Oswald, ...	634
Oswin (in Bernicia), ...⎫	
Oswine (in Deira), ...⎬	642
Oswin (sole king), ...	651
Ecgfrith, ...	670
Alchfrith, ...	685

III.

TABLE OF PRINCIPAL EVENTS.

	A.D.
Battle of Heathfield; death of Eadwin, .	633
Battle of Hefenfield, ...	634
Aidan, first Bishop of Lindisfarne, . .	635
Battle of Maserfield, ...	642
Death of Aidan, ...	651
Conversion of Peada, ...	653
Wilfrith at Rome, ...	654
Battle of Winwoed, ...	655
Monastery of Whitby founded, . . .	656
Wilfrith at Ripon, ...	661
Conference of Whitby, ...	664
Pestilence at Melrose, ...	664
Wilfrith appointed to the see of York, . .	664
Theodore, Archbishop of Canterbury, . .	669
Death of Oswin of Northumbria; Ecgfrith succeeds, ...	670

M'Farlane & Erskine, Printers, Edinburgh.

www.ingramcontent.com/pod-product-compliance
Lightning Source LLC
Chambersburg PA
CBHW030132030726
47498CB00007B/2661